BERMUDA STAR

A Ship at War

Mike Taylor

The Bermuda Star: A Ship at War

Mike Taylor

Paperback Edition First Published in the United Kingdom in 2016 by aSys Publishing

eBook Edition First Published in the United Kingdom in 2016 by aSys Publishing

Disclaimer

This is a work of fiction. Names, characters, businesses, places, events and incidents are either the products of the author's imagination or used in a fictitious manner. Any resemblance to actual persons, living or dead, or actual events is purely coincidental.

ISBN: 978-1-910757-74-1

aSys Publishing
http://www.asys-publishing.co.uk

BERMUDA STAR

The Bermuda Star is a merchant ship, at sea during World War 2. The story is about a convoy of ships transiting the Mediterranean Sea, having sailed from Devonport, in Plymouth Sound, Through the Bay of Biscay and into Gibraltar. The object of this fleet is to relieve the Island of Malta, desperately in need of food, water, ammunition, aircraft fuel, aircraft, and medicine for injured civilians and servicemen. The story of the Bermuda Star, however, goes further than Malta and into the Indian Ocean.

CHAPTER 1

BERMUDA STAR

A Ship at War

Evans arrived back in Southampton about 10:35 PM on Friday; he knew that he would not be able to do anything until Monday morning at the earliest. Nevertheless, he'd been recalled early by the company. He was not sure whether anyone would be in the company office at this time of night. He made his way to the dock gate and presented his identity card to the Police.

"You're late chief."

"Late? How can I be late? I've just got off the train – I don't understand."

"All the crew of SS Bermuda Star returned 24 hours ago. I have been told to direct you Straight on board. She's lying at number 14 berth. You'd better cut along a bit Smartly old chap." He didn't understand what the policeman meant, he wasn't late.? He made his way through the docks and along to where the ship was berthed.

As he approached the vessel, he noted the frantic activity

taking place under the bright lights of the dockside flood-lights. Cranes were busy loading large crates on board. Crates of what he knew not, but he was about to find out. He made his way up the gangway where the quartermaster was there to greet him.

"Evening Mr. Evans, you are to proceed straight to the Captain's cabin if you please Sir.

"Thank you quartermaster," said Evans. He made his way to the Captain's cabin and knocked the door; he opened the door without waiting for a reply.

"Good evening Chief," said the Captain "Sorry if you are a bit confused about events, but I had time only to send you a telegram for immediate re-call, so I was expecting you back this evening anyway, though a bit earlier than this?"

"I buried my wife yesterday afternoon; I thought you were aware of that, and I only received your telegram this morning. I am back now, however. Perhaps you would be good enough to fill me in. I can see there is some sort of emergency" said Evans.

"I've ordered the second engineer to proceed with fueling in your absence" Said Captain Royce. "We have to be out of here by 0400 in the morning, there really is no time for explanations at the moment, suffice to say that we are sailing for the Mediterranean as soon as we are loaded, fuelled and stored. I'll leave you to get about your business and talk when we're underway."

"Right Captain, I'll talk to you later then."

Evans left the Captain and went to his cabin to change. Within 10 minutes he was heading for the engine room. He found his deputy pouring over the fuelling log in the engine control room.

"Evening Tom, what's going on? I came back blissfully

unaware of any emergency. I've been on and off the damn train for about ten hours trying to get back. Two bloody air raids on the way. Luckily, we got into the Severn Tunnel just in time to avoid being hit by the first raid, but Bristol Railway Station took a few big hits. Not sure how many casualties there were," He looked vacantly at Tom Taylor, then shook his head and said, "Anyway what's the state of fuelling?"

"Glad your back chief, sorry you had such a rough time." Said Taylor. "We have just five and six bunkers left to fill, should be complete within the next hour or so."

"OK Tom, and thank you for your concern. So why all the activity? Asked Evans. "Apparently there was a panic on earlier this week, just after you left for home, The Balmoral Castle (Sister Ship of Bermuda Star), developed major problems in both of their generators and they couldn't get spares before next week. They had stripped both generators down to save time, or so they thought. Anyway, we have inherited their trip to the Med., so that puts our maintenance of number two boiler back on hold. It seems that Malta is under siege and they are desperately in need of the stuff we have been loading up. Spitfire's and spare parts for damaged aircraft, they need food and clothing in fact anything else we can carry, including ammunition. The poor old RAF are taking a hammering out there, and it seems there is little or no food left for the civilian population either."

"Why in the hell didn't someone send me a wire, I'd have been back earlier had I known?" said Evans. This statement was just frustration on Evans' part. He only buried his wife yesterday, and he was on the train back this morning.

Taylor, sensing the Chief's embarrassment said: "I don't think it was expected that we'd have to go to Malta Chief, we didn't know anything at all until late last night and you were due back today anyway."

Suddenly they heard loud explosions "Quick. Up top" said the Chief, "It sounds like another bloody air raid, as if I hadn't had enough of them today, are there any stokers down here?"

"No, they're all helping with the storing and loading."

"Let's hope there is a shelter nearby, can't afford to lose anyone now."

They rushed up to the deck to find an air raid in full swing, Southampton had taken a beating, particularly in the past few weeks. Thankfully there were not too many ships in the port, but the naval dockyard at Portsmouth was also in line of sight, and it was obviously the Prime Target on the German agenda, after crippling the Merchant Fleet lined up at Southampton docks. The two engineers took refuge in the engine-room hatchway.

"No point in running to the shelters ashore or anywhere," said Evans. As he spoke, two ratings jumped into the hatchway space beside them to dodge the bombs. They were two of the stokers that Tom had said were working with the loading crew.

"Oh, sorry Chief." said one of the men.

"Didn't seem any point in trying to find the shelter on the jetty."

"That's OK lads, looks like they've finished with us, for now anyway; carry on Tom, and I'll see what I can find out about sailing, the Skipper did mention 0400h. Maybe this raid will set us back a bit. I'll see you back in the engine room."

After the "All Clear" had sounded and the Air Raid had finished, those people who had taken refuge ashore, started to emerge from the shelters around the wharf and began to take stock of the situation. Dockyard Policemen and Wardens were running all over the place, and the sound of fire tenders was all around the jetty. Evans was very prominent in his white overalls and about to go down the gangway to see if they still had a fuel connection, he was also taking stock of any obvious external damage to the ship. He was responsible for the Damage Control and any Fire hazard which might present itself. At that moment the Captain came up behind him.

"Can you see any damage Chief I was watching from the bridge, didn't seem to be any point in going ashore, if we had been hit, it would have been all over anyway."

"I can't see any immediate damage Captain, but I'm on my way down to check that the fuel lines have been disconnected before the whole damn lot explodes."

These two men – the Senior Officers on the ship – had known each other for many years and had sailed on several ships together as young officers. However, they were not exactly friends, but they were always professional and civil.

OK Chief, I'll do the rounds on board and meet you in the wardroom", Both men went about their respective tasks.

The First Officer, Phillip Rogers, met the Engineer as he stepped off the gangway and onto the jetty. "Hello Chief," said Rogers "Caught us on the hop that time didn't it? I've been along the jetty, most of the damage has been done over by the Main Gate; it doesn't seem to have hit anywhere on this end – thank goodness."

"Hello Phil, that's a blessing then. Do we have a full complement ready to sail?"

"Yes they're all back, but the Chief Steward is ashore, still sorting out last minute business,"

"As only Chief Stewards know how," said the chief with a smile.

The chief steward was a bit of a character, a man who always seemed to get anything he needed, anything that might even have been difficult to obtain or even denied to anyone else. The arrangement suited everyone on board, and no one ever asked questions. If they did, that would have been met with a sharp nautical retort.

The Chief Steward was responsible for most of the ships stores that were being loaded, and that included food of course. He was good at his job and provided a good food table for the whole ship's crew. He was the most popular man on board.

After inspecting the ship from the jetty, both the Engineer and First Officer confirmed that there was no structural damage and fuelling had been completed satisfactorily. They walked back up the gangway together, and as they reached the top, they turned to see a red van pulling up and out jumped the Chief Steward.

"Anyone up there to give me a hand loading stores please chief." The steward shouted.

He turned to the back of the vehicle, opened the door, and began to unload a whole van full of fresh vegetables, fruit, and other goodies which were not visible.

The chief officer detailed several ratings to go and assist the steward, then both he and the Engineer proceeded to the wardroom to meet with the Captain. All the Officers were assembled in the Wardroom (that is the officers dining room, and recreation space) – for a briefing from the Captain. There was a knock on the door, and one of the junior officers opened it to reveal the Chief Steward. At that point, the Captain looked up.

"Ah, come in Mr. Summers, this concerns you too" (I should ruddy hope so too) he said to himself, under his breath.

The Captain then turned to the assembled officers. "Gentlemen," he said "Most of you will know roughly what we are about to undertake and I want you to understand that it will not be a picnic. Malta is under siege and in the thick of the war. We, along with a number of other vessels, will be proceeding to Plymouth Sound, sailing from Southampton at about 0400h, there we will be joining convoy H22 who have been assembling for the past week. We will then sail – in convoy – and under escort from the Royal Navy, down through the Bay of Biscay to Gibraltar."

Captain Royce had a way of making these announcements sound as if he were addressing a large congregation in church. He was a lay preacher and a severe man in command. (He continued): "On arrival in Gibraltar we will await our further instructions. It is known that the final destination; Malta, is under heavy attack on a daily basis, and I do not anticipate A long stay in port. There will be no time for anything other than fuelling and the collection of any mail etc. We have a small contingent of Royal Navy personnel on board under the orders of Lieutenant Thompson here," (Thompson acknowledged with a nod). "You will have noticed that several pieces of armament have been installed, not the least of which are two heavy machine guns on the Port and Starboard side of the bridge. These guns will be handled by the Navy initially, but it is my intention to familiarise selected crew members with the task of backup to the Naval Gunners – or – Armourers. In the event, they can take over from the Navy in an emergency ".

He made this announcement with a peculiar sneer it

seemed to the onlookers, as he continued his speech: "This should tell you that this trip could be more hazardous than any previous voyage we have ever undertaken. Our task is quite clear: We will deliver the goods!

He looked around at the attentive faces to see what impact his words had made, and went on to say—

"I expect that every man on board will do his duty . . .

"Who does he think he is, Bloody Nelson" One of the junior officers spoke out of the corner of his mouth, to his equally junior comrade standing alongside him at the back of the room.

The Captain glared at the offender, and carried on . . . "To do his duty in the time-honoured way – for King and Country. Thank you, gentlemen, for your attention, I will meet with all seaman officers now on the bridge."

He left the wardroom, quickly followed by the Chief Officer, who was the second in command. The Radio Officer managed to give a swift kick in the backside to the young cadet who made the remark about Nelson during the Captain's speech. The remaining officers included the engine room, the Royal Naval lieutenant and the Steward, who in true seamanship fashion said – "Who would like what to drink before we sail? This is The Last Chance Saloon."

They all looked at Rowland Evans.

"Yes please, Stew. I'll have a drop of scotch."

Evans went straight over to the Naval Officer.

"Good evening Lieutenant," he said, offering his hand to shake, "I'm Rowland Evans the Chief Engineer, anything I can do to assist, please ask."

"Thank you chief, – Gordon Thompson," he said shaking Evans' hand.

"It's been a bit hectic for all of us at such short notice,

and with more trauma to come, I fear. I'll be glad to answer any queries – except why I'm here," He said with a grin, and turned and left the wardroom. The remaining officers were now able to relax – temporarily.

The Chief Engineer was senior officer present and had set a precedent for The remaining officers, by accepting the Steward's invitation for a drink. During the short respite, each man was able to take stock of his own personal situation, and reflect on his lot, some, with apprehension; some with resignation and all taking a short breather from the task in hand.

"When did you get back Taff?" said Evans to Summers—

The Chief Engineer reserved this little familiarity for the Chief Steward.

They were both from South Wales and had known each other for many years.

"I got in the night before last, I had a lot to do, and it was just as well I started early, I haven't stopped loading provisions since I got back. I think the Skipper must have got wind of this situation before I came back you know. He was certainly well up on the requirements for fuel and everything. Now that's not normally his way, is it? And I don't think he's taken too kindly to the Royal Navy being on board either."

"No, it makes me wonder why he didn't re-call me earlier," Evans said – "Though I could not have got back any earlier, and I had a hell of a trip as it happened anyway."

"Yeah' I heard, and there was an air raid over Swansea Docks again before I left, that was the day before you," said Summers.

"Well I didn't want to hang around, Evans said "I have nothing left at home now since Margaret was killed. My daughter lives down in West Wales so they should be far enough away from the raids on Swansea Docks, not to be too much of a worry."

"I heard about your wife Rowland; I'm so sorry. I'm sorry also that I couldn't make it to her funeral. I didn't even know about it until I got to the station to get on the train, Graham Jones the ticket inspector told me, I was on my way back by then."

"Not to worry Taff – it was just family anyway, and only six of them." Evans looked away. The steward could feel his grief, so he said nothing, He slowly poured another whiskey into Rowland's glass, placed the bottle back on the shelf behind the bar and walked out of the wardroom.

The remaining ship's officers, also realising the chief engineer's grief, left the wardroom and went to their respective places of duty. There was frantic activity taking place to get the ship ready to sail; Dave Summers went to find the Chief chef to talk about provisions and discuss menus for the coming weeks at sea.

CHAPTER 2

They sailed from Southampton at 04:00 on Tuesday morning, and arrived to join the convoy in Plymouth Sound at around 09:00. Captain Royce reported their arrival to the Port Authority and was allocated an anchorage. Before he could work out where he was supposed to go, the Pilot Cutter came alongside with a local Pilot and a Royal Naval Commander. Royce would never admit it, but he had no idea where the allocated anchorage was, He was relieved to hand the responsibility to the local Pilot to bring him to his berth. He was not, however; prepared for the next stage of the proceedings, when he was ordered politely to the wardroom along with all crew members who could be spared, including six naval ratings, the Chief Engineer, the Chief Officer and their immediate subordinates, and the Radio Officers. Cdr. Frank Trail, the Royal Navy Commander, addressed the assembled crew.

"Gentlemen, I must first apologise to Capt. Royce" he nodded to the Captain. "for my unorthodox arrival, but it is essential that my presence on board remains unannounced, hence boarding with the pilot. My presence on board should not concern anyone at this time, suffice to say that when we run into the enemy on passage – and we will, it will become clear why I am here. A number of items of deck cargo will be loaded on board within the next half hour or so and will be secured on the after end of the cargo hold hatches." Addressing the Chief Engineer, he said; "I trust Chief that the hatch covers will hold the weight of some boxes? I'll go into it with you when this meeting is finished."

He turned back to the assembled crew.

"Make no mistake we are going into a war zone, but you will have known that. The enemy will be attacking us right from the start and you will have guessed that also. But what you will not have guessed is that this convoy is crucial to the outcome of the war. You will no doubt have heard on the B.B.C. News that the Island of Malta is under heavy attack on a daily basis, in fact three or four times a day some of the time. Both the military and the civilian population are suffering severe casualties. The RAF is flying valiant defensive attacks around the clock, but they are running out of aircraft, ammunition – and men – on all fronts. The German's are attacking from North Africa, they are also attacking from Egypt, not once or twice, but continuously, day in day out. Malta is crucial to the outcome of the war and must be defended at all cost, so you see how important you all are to the war effort. They need the contents of, not just this ship, but of every ship in the convoy, each one is carrying a life-saving cargo, whether it is food, oil, or weapons, and every ship is bent on reaching the same destination. Make no mistake; the enemy will make every effort to stop this convoy, and I expect them to use every means at their disposal to achieve their end result, this includes U-boat, aircraft, and surface warship attack. There will be no let-up during the whole of this trip, especially down through the Bay of

Biscay where we will be vulnerable to – both the elements, as well as the enemy. Once we enter the Mediterranean at Gibraltar, I would hope that we can pull into the naval Base to refuel and replenish anything we may need. However, that is NOT a certainty. Gibraltar is also vulnerable to attack; though not quite so obvious since it is part of neutral Spain, but of course, still British Territory. You may rest assured; there will be agents in Gibraltar, especially in the Dockyard, who will be trying to elicit information from anyone who is foolish enough to speak out of turn. So remember the old saying — "LOOSE LIPS SINK SHIPS" . . . and as dramatic as that may sound; the enemy will be trying to second guess our destination. They will not be certain of it, but they all know that Malta is under siege conditions. So be aware of the Dockyard Matey, and any others who appear to be overly pleasant, and inquisitive about our movements. I trust gentlemen that I have given you all food for thought, I will not be available for questions after this meeting, I have told you everything you need to know, and thank you for your time."

With that Trail picked up his cap and walked out of the room, leaving everyone speechless, and pondering the abrupt manner the Royal Navy had imparted the information they had all been waiting to hear.

The Chief Officer stepped forward at that point and said – "Watch-keepers to anchor watches and departments to your stations – Heads of departments, please see me after you have completed your duties."

He also picked up his cap and walked out of the wardroom leaving Captain Royce looking bewildered, as everyone else dispersed to their various departments. The wind had been taken out of Royce's sails, and he was left alone to ponder as he sat alone in the wardroom. He had not even gone to his own spacious cabin after the dispersal of the crew. When, Suddenly, the wardroom door opened and the Chief Officer came in.

"Captain, are you all right? I have been looking for you to tell you that we have gone to anchor stations, and we are about to embark."

"Who gave that order?"

Royce spluttered getting to his feet. "Cdr. Trail gave the order about half an hour ago; I sent a messenger to your cabin; he returned to say you were not there . . . He trailed off as the Captain exploded into action.

"How dare he order my ship to up anchor, how dare he do anything without my permission?" Royce moved to the door and brushed the First Officer aside as he made his way to the bridge. On arrival on the bridge, Royce seemed to be confused and shouted for Rogers, who was right behind him.

"Right Rogers," the Captain had never called his chief officer by his surname before.

"I want to see that Navy Lieutenant, go and bring him to the bridge."

"I am a Royal Navy Commander, Captain," Said a voice. Trail had been standing at the back of the bridge as Royce had arrived – "And I have to tell you that I am in overall command of this ship. You will please refrain from shouting and get this vessel under way; I shall speak with you in private when we are settled into steaming watches."

Royce was left fuming by this 'put-down, he had no choice but to give the order to – "Up anchor Chief Officer, take the ship to sea, I'll be in my cabin" he said, and left the bridge. Although he was more than qualified to obey the order, Rogers was not only surprised but disturbed, by the Captain's action and his general attitude, it was the Captain's responsibility to be on the bridge when the ship put to sea, as laid down in Company Orders, and seamanship generally. He was about to make an entry into the Ship's Log when Trail came to look over his shoulder.

"Don't make an entry in the log Mr. Rogers," He said in a low voice, "The Captain is required to read Admiralty Instructions on sailing, and he has gone to do so in his cabin, maybe he should have informed you of his intention, but he is a bit confused about my presence at the moment. If you have any questions at all, please refer them to me. I will explain things to you in more detail when we have settled down to the routine. Thank you for your co-operation and acceptance of the situation. I'll talk to you later."

The Fist Officer mumbled; "thank you, Sir," and even in his bewilderment, he was first and last, the ship's most senior officer next to the Chief engineer, and he had a ship to run.

"Who is the Officer of the Watch please?" he asked loudly . . . He was very embarrassed by the Captain's remarks, but he disguised his feelings as he took the ship through the routine of going sea. A job he had trained for during his advancement, and hoped, of one day becoming a Captain of his own ship. He dismissed the remarks as unwarranted.

"Officer of the Watch, Steer south by southwest"

"Steer South by southwest, Aye-Aye Sir."

During the next hours from the departure from Plymouth, the whole ship's company was busy within their own departments, and working watches as normal. Their task was not as easy as sailing alone like they normally did, they were now in convoy, and Rogers had not yet been informed of the intentions for the convoy disposition These instructions, were in the letter that Cdr. Trail had given to Royce as soon as he had boarded, and the Captain had not thought fit to read, before turning over the bridge to the first officer. There were more complicated manoeuvres needed to bring a large number of ships into the English Channel even if it were the widest part before entering the Atlantic Ocean. "Messenger" Rogers called, "Yes Sir."

"Please find Cdr. Trail and ask him if he would kindly come to the bridge He may be in Radio Room."

"Aye – Aye Sir"

Trail appeared within minutes. Phillip, how can I help you?"

Rogers was slightly taken aback by the familiarity; he was warmed by the approach.

"Yes Sir, I'm not sure of my position in regard to convoy disposition, I'm afraid I have seen nothing to advise where I should be."

"Yes no problem I was just setting things up in the radio room," said Trail.

"One of my ratings will be working with your operators to establish contact with the Flag Officer in HMS. Camperdown, I'll plug a loudspeaker through to the bridge, so you can listen in to the chatter, I must find out if the Captain is all clued up, He had rather a lot to read through. Meanwhile, maintain present heading until we get the nod from Camperdown. OK?"

"Yes, thank you, sir."

"And less of the Sir," said Trail with a wink as he went off to find the Captain.

Royce's attitude disturbed Cdr. Trail. He had no intention of trying to undermine the Captain's authority on board his own ship; but Royce seemed reluctant to appreciate the importance of the Royal Navy's presence on board; even though soon after leaving Plymouth, Trail had given the Bermuda Star's Captain a secret envelope directing him to co-operate Fully with the Naval officer in charge, and to comply with that officer's every order. It was also made clear to Royce, that even though his ship may be in danger during attack from enemy ships and aircraft, he was to seek advice in any situation from the Royal Navy Commander. In other words, Trail was in command outside of day to day running of the ship.

Royce was sitting in his cabin. After his angry departure from the bridge, he decided to let the outburst lie for the moment. His pride had been bruised. He had not opened the envelope that the Navy Commander had given him, stubbornly brushing aside any interference from the Royal Navy, He knew however, they were in for a rough ride in the next weeks, and he needed maximum co-operation from the ship's crew to achieve his own ends.

He decided to read the instructions passed on to him from the Admiralty and endorsed by the Company the reading of which gave him no satisfaction, except to further his anger and frustration; as he resolved to maintain his own command of the Bermuda Star. At that moment there was a knock on the door. Before any answer was given, Trail walked into the Captain's suite; a spacious room with a large table and eight chairs around it, now covered in charts and navigational books, none of which had been used by the Captain for a number of hours. However, anything he had charted was now irrelevant.

"Captain," said Cdr. Trail "Forgive the intrusion, but we must look at the situation presenting itself to us in the next half hour. I have brought the relevant charts and if you would kindly clear the table, of your previous endeavour, we will get down to the business of sailing this convoy, in complete safety, to Gibraltar." With a face like thunder, Royce cleared the table Trail spread the new charts out "Now Captain, the disposition of the convoy is ...

CHAPTER 3

During the passage down channel and out into the Atlantic Ocean, the Naval gun crews had been working hard on their equipment, testing the two guns on either side of the bridge, and several other small arms, a Sten gun, and two heavy machine guns, which slotted into brackets fitted on each side of the bridge deck. They also sorted out the ammunition lockers and brought the 'ammo up from the deck that their boss – Cdr. Trail, had stowed on the hatch covers when they came on board. During the course of the day, the gun's crews had also taken the time to give some instruction to the four hands from Bermuda Star who had been designated as spare guns' crew, at the Captain's insistence and Cdr. Trail's approval.

Lieut. Thompson, who was the gunnery officer, had undertaken to train four suitably able civilian crew members in gunnery instruction.

He was impressed by the willingness and the common sense shown by the men chosen to become "Gunners", and was satisfied that under fire, and in an emergency, they would perform their duty with professionalism, and live up to the responsibility expected of them. He put them under the guidance of his Petty Officer and the six naval ratings, they all got on well together.

By nightfall on Wednesday the convoy was well out into the Atlantic Ocean and was spreading out over a large area – some 5 to 10 miles between them, with the slowest ships nearest the land to the East, and the faster ships to seaward. Even at this early stage in their perilous voyage – west into the Atlantic, Then South into the Bay of Biscay, Lieut. Thompson knew that they would all have to prove their worth before very long.

It was a long trip out into the Atlantic, with the escorting Naval ships trying to herd the slower civilian-manned vessels along and to keep some sort of shape in the convoy. The added danger of U-boats became more and more acute as they staggered along at speeds which were as low as eight to ten knots, and it was not long before the first U-boat attacks began.

On Thursday morning a contact was picked up by one of the destroyers out on the most westerly part of the convoy. A message was sent to the Long Range Maritime Patrol HQ at Plymouth, to report the contact, and two aircraft, already covering the convoy were given the information. The warships' asdic operators were working overtime to track the enemy submarine, and so far, one of the destroyers had managed to drop depth charges in the area thought to be the target submarine, they were joined by one of the two long-range RAF aircraft, who also dropped charges. But this coverage from the RAF would not last much longer due to the distance between land, the Fleet's journey south, and the aircraft distance from home before running out of fuel.

Somehow the convoy got away with this early attack, but the enemy submarine was not actually seen to surface, so she was either sunk or had got away. If she had escaped, It would not be long before the area of the convoy had been passed on to other German submarines, that may be in the area.

Hours later it was obvious she had got away. The attack on the convoy intensified, both from the U-boats and two enemy aircraft who had joined in the attack from the air.

Fortunately these air attacks caused little damage, and the enemy aircraft retired early, due to fuel loss it was presumed, but by day six on their southerly voyage, the convoy had lost one merchant ship, and, one of the Navy's corvettes to enemy torpedoes from a submarine. The first attacks on the convoy came from the air, the gun crews had been closed up at Action Stations for hours, both the guns on either side of the bridge had been in action, and had performed well, the civilian gunners had proved to be keen and enthusiastic under fire from the enemy. But by the time Gibraltar hove into view, and after days of intensive attack from the enemy, another merchant vessel had been lost to submarine attack. Some survivors had been picked up by the Navy, but in the heavy seas prevailing in the Bay of Biscay, it was a task, almost impossible to hope for that all survivors would be found, especially in that area. One of the escorting destroyers had been detached from the convoy to search the vast sea and look for further Survivors, HMS Barfleur, A destroyer, designated to the job of herding the slower merchant ships, finally arrived in Gibraltar two days after the main force, having picked up only 26 men from the ships that had been destroyed by the enemy. By that time the convoy had reached and anchored in the Gibraltar "Roads." Exhausted, and needing fuel and stores. Each ship had to wait its turn to re-fuel and store up, and there were a large number of other ships anchored in the Bay, also awaiting stores, fuel, and further instructions? Among the ships anchored in the roads, and those tied up alongside in the docks, were a number of Royal Navy ships, including two Aircraft Carriers. The Bermuda Star had been given an anchorage close-in towards the Gibraltar Harbour entrance.

Dave Summers, the chief steward, had a list as long as your arm of stores he needed to get from ashore. However, the naval commander could not yet give any permission to go ashore, even he was unable to go to the Admiralty Office in the dockyard. He had been ordered to stay put until further orders. Later, while the crew were waiting for instructions, (But instructions for what?). The Chief Steward and Rowland Evans were leaning over the guard rail and looking in towards the 'Rock.'

"Never changes, does it Taff?" said Evans.

"It's stood the test of time and no mistake; I admit to having a soft spot for the old place."

Summers said. "Yes, you know 'The Trocadero very well, (A well-known Pub) no doubt, and its dancing girls eh Taff?"

"Who me chief?" said Summers in mock, shock horror.

"I do need to go ashore, though; as soon as we can, and I know you have to go as well, but no doubt you have enough fuel?"

"Yes, it's not fuel but spares I need, for one of my generators. I couldn't get anything in Southampton before we sailed. I'd better go and see if there is any change in the routine yet, I don't want to hang around all day."

I must say, I like Cdr. Trail" said the steward "He's a straight talker alright. I'm still worried about the 'Old Man, though." This, was a reference to the Captain's strange behaviour since they had sailed from Plymouth Sound.

"He has hardly spoken to me the whole trip," said

Summers, "most odd, he seems to have left the whole of the running of the ship to the Navy and poor old Phillip Rogers. It would not surprise me if he is questioned by the Company before long. It does not make for a happy situation especially in the present circumstance."

The chief engineer did not want to be drawn into any discussion along those lines, and he said, "I'm just off now to the engine room. See you later Taff, and I'd keep all that to myself if I were you."

Left alone again, Summers reflected, that perhaps he should not have confided in a senior officer, it wasn't done, especially if it concerned the Captain. He went off to his own little world, first stopping at the wardroom to talk to his junior.

"Make sure that the Captain has his dinner served up in his cabin: I don't want him in the mess with the rest of the officers."

"Too late chief," said the junior steward "He's gone Ashore, he went in the Navy Patrol Boat when they brought the mail on board.

I don't know if anyone else saw him go, it was just chance that I saw him, he sort of sneaked onto the patrol boat.

"I doubt that Smithy, he was off to see the Port Captain about our sailing orders I expect. Now off you go and don't say anything about this to anyone else – OK?" "Yeah OK Chief, but it did seem odd to me."

With that the steward went on his way, leaving Summers wondering if he should say anything to the Naval Commander. He decided to leave it lie for the moment. but he knew there was trouble brewing somewhere, and it disturbed him.

Just after one o' clock and whilst the officers were about

to start their lunch, the ship's Captain barged into the ward-room and shouted, at no one in particular,

"This is MY SHIP! He raged, "And let no one forget it,"

Then he turned about and left the room, banging the wardroom door, and leaving everyone agog.

"Gentlemen" Cdr. Trail, who had been dining with the ship's officers, said "It is obvious that the Captain has had some sort of upset. Please acknowledge that he is not himself. I will go and see if I can find out what is wrong."Trail left the room and proceeded to the Captain's cabin. He knocked on the door and waited for a reply.

When no answer was forthcoming, he tried the door and had intended to enter the room uninvited; however the door was locked, so he knocked, and said – through the closed door. "Captain this is Commander Trail, please allow me to speak with you."There was no reply. Trail knocked once more and waited, but still no reply from within, so he left and returned to the wardroom, where all officers were still seated and eating, expectantly waiting to hear what Trail had to say.

"Please carry on with lunch gentlemen."

"Mr. Evans, could I see you on the bridge when you have finished with lunch please, No rush."

Evans looked at the other officers at the table.

"I don't like the look of this," He said.

He pushed his plate away, excused himself from the table, and went out of the room.

"I wonder what all that was about," The junior radio officer said.

"Just get on with your dinner," said the second engineer, "and mind your own business."

With that everyone at the table pushed their plates away,

stood up and left the room leaving the radio officer alone in the wardroom.

Evans proceeded to the bridge to talk to Trail. He found him to be in an unusually pensive mood, or so it seemed. "Ah, chief, he said, let us go outside."

Evans said nothing and followed the commander out onto the bridge deck.

"I'm finding this business with the Captain very disturbing, especially in the present circumstances. I'm afraid it is affecting the officers particularly, and will eventually cause the crew some anxiety also, I hope I can count on your support when I go inboard to see the Admiral about the remainder of our voyage to Malta? It is going to be a very testing journey, much worse than the one we have just encountered possibly."

"I have sailed with Mr. Royce many times commander", said Evans.

"We were junior midshipmen together a long time ago. I must admit I have never seen him in such a state as he is at the moment. He has been a dedicated Christian all of his life, and not always easy to please, but this is unusual. What is it you would like me to do if a situation arises?", He asked Trail.

"We already have a situation chief, and it is not one that I would want to have on the next leg of our journey. We have a cargo on board which is essential to the lives of the people of Malta and our own serving personnel. I shall convey my concerns to the authority inboard, which is why I would be grateful to have you along – even to express your own concerns – if any, about the Captain's capability – in his present condition, and what effect that may have on the ships company."

"Well," said Evans, "I would not like to condemn the Captain for any untoward misconduct; or anything of the like. He may just have had difficulty in accepting the Royal Navy to completely take over the running of his ship, as I suspect would any Captain. Given the circumstances, however, I would gladly come with you and convey my concerns about his recent behaviour, especially if it will help him personally, but I have no intention of belittling the Captain in his present state."

"I can assure you, Mr. Evans; there will be no belittling on my part, but you must see that I have no choice but to address the facts as I see them. I have a boat ready alongside if you are ready Please Chief?"

They both embarked on the boat and proceeded forthwith to the command offices ashore. They were immediately conveyed to the Admiral's office. As they entered, the WREN secretary stood up and said – "This way gentlemen The Admiral is expecting you."

She opened the Admiral's, door and announced—

"Cdr. Trail for you sir."

"Come in gentlemen; please be seated."

Turning to Evans he said, "You will be the chief engineer, Mr. Evans"? Offering his hand to shake.

"Yes, thank you, Admiral." Turning to Trail, the Admiral asked—

"Now then Commander, how can I help?"

"Sir, when I boarded the Bermuda Star at Devonport," he began "I did so under cover of the tug delivering mail, I was trying to remain inconspicuous of course. I proceeded to the wardroom, where all the officers, including the Captain, were assembled, and I laid out the procedure for the forthcoming trip to Malta. The ship was being loaded with equipment, mainly weapons, and ammunition. I then outlined the procedure that I required from the ship's company, including the Captain, – and my men, in the defense of the ship against attack, from both the air and possible – no – PROBABLE – submarine attack. I'm afraid the Captain's reaction to this was uncooperative, or so it seemed, I outlined the necessary precautions with my team on board, and that it would be helpful if some members of the ship's company could be trained up with the gun's crew to assist them. This was agreed immediately, I must admit, I am completely baffled by Captain Royce's behaviour since. He has now locked himself in his cabin and refuses to speak to me.

The Admiral turned to Evans and asked, "What do you make of this chief?"

"I must admit Admiral I don't know what to make of it. Captain Royce and I go back to very young ship's officer's, in our cadet days. He is a very religious man, a lay preacher, though, I don't remember him ever bringing that on board – except for the usual Sunday church service at sea, for those who wished to attend. He and I both have our own ways of course and we seldom – these days anyway – mix socially. I'm afraid I don't know what to make of it. As a Captain at sea and in command of his ship I can't fault him."

"Thank you chief," said the Admiral.

"I think that is all I can ask of you, a straight answer, and loyalty to your Captain.

You may return to your engine room now and get among your engines, thank you again. Next time we meet I hope we have a gin and tonic in our hands."

The Admiral extended his hand and shook Evans's hand," good luck old man," he said with a smile.

Evans said, "Thank you Admiral, and good luck to you sir."

He left the room, and saying goodbye to the pretty little wren at her desk, he went off across the dockyard, to try to get a boat back to his ship. He had no idea what the outcome of the meeting would be after he left Trail in the Admiral's office. He had no doubt, however, that Royce's position would now be under some scrutiny.

Evans was lucky enough to get a lift from one of the runabout boats, which were back and for to the anchored ships. He returned on board Bermuda Star and went directly to the wardroom. A few of the officers were having a short break. And Evans went straight to the teapot and poured himself a cup of tea; knowing that, before long, he would be questioned about the outcome of the visit ashore. He sat at the table and said "Before you ask, I have no idea what is going to happen to the Captain, but rest assured; we will be sailing very soon, with or without him, that's all I can say, for now, we must wait and see. He finished his cup of tea and left the wardroom for the engine room.

Just at the moment, no one had any idea when the ship would sail in convoy, or even if they had a Captain, it was very awkward to know what was to happen next. Meanwhile, the crew went about their duties as normal.

At about five o clock the naval commander returned on board. He sought out the Captain, who was still locked in his cabin and not answering anyone. Trail was not having any of it. He called for the second engineer and told him to bring a large wrench to the door of the Captain's cabin. When it arrived, Trail said,

"Now everybody stand back," He said loudly, "I'm going to prize the door off its hinges to make sure the Captain is still alive."

Suddenly the door opened, and the Captain emerged, "What is going on here?" he demanded.

"Ah! Captain, I was about to knock your door down, we had no idea if you were alive or dead, and we need to get the ship underway to catch up with the rest of the fleet." This of course, was not the actual truth, but Trail was determined to get Royce to measure up to his responsibility as the Captain, and get his ship underway – now.

The Captain pushed his way past the two ratings that Trail had engaged as his henchmen, and made his way in haste to the bridge, Trail followed him close behind. When the Captain entered the bridge, he was met by the Admiral.

"Good evening Captain. You will no doubt be surprised to see me? I have to tell you that I have been appointed Senior officer of the fleet, and Bermuda Star, has been appointed as my Flag Ship to that fleet until we reach Malta.

Commander Trail will be in overall command of the operation and will keep you up to date. Now you will please get the ship underway and set our course for Malta. I have ordered the fleet also to get underway, and you will lead at the head of the convoy, Are you happy with that Captain?"

"Yes indeed Admiral"

Royce appeared to be overwhelmed by the order, and began his duty as Captain of his own ship once more.

"All hands to stations for leaving harbour – anchor party raise anchor."

The shout came from the anchor crew,

"Anchor secured."

"Full ahead both engines," said Royce.

"Full ahead both engines" The helmsman repeated the order and the ship began to move ahead, much to the relief of everyone on board it appeared.

"I will discuss my accommodation with the chief steward Captain, you will retain your own quarters, of course. Commander Trail, would you please accompany me to the wardroom. Captain – You have the bridge."

"I have the bridge Admiral – Thank you." Said Royce.

When the Admiral and Trail got to the wardroom, there were two people there; The Chief Steward and the radio officer. The radio officer got up first and left the room quickly. The chief steward asked if they would like a drink.

"Tea? – Coffee, or something stronger Gentlemen?"

"A nice cup of Tea I think Mr. Summers said the Admiral."

With that, the two senior officers relaxed in the comfort of the wardroom lounge. When the steward returned, he placed a small table in front of the officers, and placed a tray, containing cups and saucers, a tray of sandwiches and two plates.

"That should warm you up a bit Admiral.

Dinner will probably be a little later this evening gentlemen; I should hope to be about 20:00."

"Thank you, Taff, said Trail," with a wink.

The steward then left the room.

"Now then commander, we have our work cut out to organize this fleet. We have one Aircraft Carrier, and four Destroyers plus one Frigate added to our fleet. I'm hoping to raise a few more Gunners, and possibly at least two more escorts, I won't know exactly, until I can get a nod from my relief, who of course only came to relieve me of command yesterday. My presence seems to be needed more in Malta, for some reason. We must now decide the disposition of this convoy. We need to position the slower Merchant vessels, especially the big oil carrier, we now have in the fleet. She has been loaded here In Gibraltar. Don't ask me how. Suffice to say she is now with us for protection. I intend to keep the destroyers as close as we can to the Oil Tanker. It will not be easy of course, but she is a very important commodity, perhaps more so than some of the other ships, although, they are all carrying vital food and equipment, it means we will have our work cut out. The RAF will need that fuel desperately by now; I'm sure of it."

"I have been thinking of that sir," said Trail, "Would it be advisable to keep the aircraft carrier towards the north coast of Africa, so that she can shield the merchant fleet with her aircraft should the need arise?

"It had crossed my mind, John."

Trail was startled by the Admiral calling him by his Christian name.

"But I want to be able to attack the enemy with those aircraft, as soon as we get close enough to get them in the air. In fact, I was about to suggest we detach the Carrier with all haste toward Malta, to intercept the enemy before they get to the Island, a bit of a long shot maybe, but I think that, although she is not carrying more than ten aircraft, due to the load of other essentials for the Island, she will be faster alone, and it is unlikely that German planes would be expecting British fighters under the present circumstance. There is no doubt that the Carrier is the fastest ship in the fleet. And whilst I appreciate your concern for the convoy, the Islanders – and that includes our own Ground and Air Forces of course, will no longer be able to defend the Island at all if we cannot reach them with more guns and ammunition. The speed which we are able to achieve, with this convoy, will not be enough to relieve Malta soon enough."

"Of course Sir, I will instigate the Carriers departure from the fleet, directly we finish this meeting.

It was at that moment that the Chief Steward came back into the room.

"I would like to lay up for dinner if you gentlemen have finished. It will only take me a minute."

"Yes, certainly Mr. Summers," said Cdr. Trail "Have you informed the Captain?"

"Yes Sir, he is on his way down. Would you like to be seated?

"I think we will await his arrival steward."

Just at that moment, Captain Royce walked into the room.

He gave a peculiar smile at the Admiral and Cdr. Trail.

"Right Chief Steward, what have you got for us tonight? Something very tempting I hope."

The steward stood at the head of the table, holding the Captain's chair for him. He sat down, followed by the Admiral and Cdr. Trail. The steward presented the meal with his typical courtesy and aplomb. The meal included a sweet, and cheeses with cream crackers, etc. and of course coffee. The trio sat through dinner, and no one spoke a word.

"Is there anything else I can get for you, gentlemen? Summers asked when they had finished their meal.

At that very moment, a loud bang rocked the ship.

"We're under attack" shouted Royce, falling sideways in his chair and onto the floor in his haste get up quickly. The Admiral and the Commander had not seen this, as they both rose from the table and dashed out of the cabin door, heading for the bridge. The steward did not see the Captain fall over either, as he also headed out to his battle station.

As the steward dashed to his post, he heard the unmistakable sound of the ship's guns firing at the enemy aircraft attacking the fleet.

The two senior naval officers were by now on the bridge.

Commander Trail was in the Wireless office, trying to make contact with the leading destroyer to assess the situation within the fleet which was now very scattered. The destroyers were having their work cut out Marshalling the convoy, and trying to divert the attention of enemy aircraft on these vulnerable merchant ships.

The raid was having its toll on all ships, including the four destroyers and two frigates.

On board the Flagship, as Bermuda Star was now known, the gunners were frantically loading and firing on both sides of the bridge, and also from the large "Bofors gun."

on the main deck above the hold.

The Admiral and Cdr. Trail, were both now back on the bridge, Trail turned to the Admiral, and, said I'll be in the Radar room, sir! and disappeared off the bridge.

The Admiral had now taken control of the bridge from Royce, who had appeared but seemed to be unsure of what he should be doing. Two junior officers also on the bridge were looking to the Admiral for instructions.

On seeing these two bewildered junior officers wanting to help, but didn't know what they should be doing, or where they should be. The Admiral turned to them.

"Right you two. You" he said, pointing a finger at the nearest one to him. "I want you to go down to the Bofors deck and see if they need a hand with anything Come back to me when this is over – GO."

"You," he pointed at the other young officer. "Check the gun crews on both gun decks port and starboard. Lend a hand with whatever they need."

"Aye, Aye Sir," said number two who also saluted the Admiral and dashed away. There was obviously a lot going on, on the bridge, but the Admiral could see nothing now of the ship's Captain.

"Where is the Captain?" The Admiral shouted, did you see where he went, messenger?

"I think he went for'ard, Sir. What The bleeding hell – what was that" Shouted the helmsman," above all the noise. He looked at the Admiral—

"Sorry sir, that small ship came right out of the smoke. He was lucky I didn't hit him."

"Right helmsman, let's do this together. If I don't see it and you do, act accordingly OK?'

"OK sir – I suggest going to port – port wheel on – twenty degrees sir."

"Port wheel on. Ease to ten degrees, ease to ten – ten degrees on." Said the helmsman.

Trail came back onto the bridge after checking the bow, and said "That was close, but he didn't hit us – thank goodness."

By now the Admiral was standing next to the helmsman, looking out ahead. There was a lot of gun smoke from both guns on the poop deck, and from the heavier gun above the deck hatch.

"Starboard thirty helmsman – bring her round quickly"

"Starboard thirty, – thirty of starboard wheel on sir."

"Steady as she goes – now – midship's" the Admiral shouted aloud.

"Wheel amid-ships, sir,"

As they came around to mid-ships sharply, the helmsman struggled to bring the ship upright he finally succeeding with his struggle, and mumbled to himself – that was close.

"You did very well then helmsman. What's your name?"

"Watts" He said with a wide grin.

"I said What's your name?" said the Admiral again, this time, he shouted.

"Yes! – It's Watt's Sir" he said, still with a grin.

"Good job it wasn't Ball then," said the Admiral with an equally wide grin?

"I should think the Captain went to check the bow," He turned to the bridge messenger.

"See if you can find out where the Captain is please."

"Ay Ay Sir"

By this time it appeared, the aircraft pounding was easing up; the enemy aircraft seemed to have disappeared. It was obvious that a lot of damage had been caused by the air attack.

At that moment Cdr. Trail came onto the bridge. "I have been in contact with the lead Destroyer Sir, we have taken a lot of flak in the fleet, and there's a lot of damage all round.

The TANKER has taken a heavy pounding, with a lot of casualties among the crew, she is still afloat, thank goodness but listing heavily. I suggest we try to get closer to her to assess the damage. We seem to have got away with it, for the most part, no casualties here, a couple of hits back aft, but nothing too serious."

"What is our position now, and how far to go to Malta?" asked the Admiral.

"We have about a hundred miles to go to reach Malta.

If we can maintain enough speed, we might be able to make it by late afternoon tomorrow, but that's a big might. I have still to assess the damage in all areas; the wireless office is trying to make contact with the Guard Ships to find out how we can best assist" he said. This was a reference to the oil tanker, of course.

"Right," said the Admiral "Let's go and find out for

ourselves, she is too valuable to lose. Any idea of her position?

"We've tracked her on radar sir, she is about five miles astern, and listing heavily to starboard,"

"Starboard Thirty, Mr. Watts, said the Admiral, let's find our lost sheep."

"Starboard thirty Admiral" repeated the helmsman.

Trail had to smile at the obvious repartee between the helmsman and the Admiral.

"Commander, see if you can find Captain Royce please, he has been missing for at least an hour or more. Ask him to come to the bridge and sail his ship, would you?

"Certainly sir," Trail said.

Trail went back into the radar room to detail one of the crew, to seek out the Captain and tell him his presence was required on the bridge immediately. Meanwhile, the radio room had contacted the Tanker, informing them that help was on its way, and asking what their position was.

Back on the bridge, the Admiral seemed to be enjoying himself, being in charge of a ship again. But there had been no sign of the Captain, and this was causing concern for Commander Trail. He had two of the crew searching for him now, and he had to leave them to it.

The Bermuda Star had finally caught up to the crippled tanker. One of the destroyers was holding the huge ship up, on the starboard side. That ship was Barfleur, who had been responsible for saving the lives of some of the ships' crews in the Atlantic, on the way down to Gibraltar. The crew of the destroyer were now assisting, the injured sailors on the Tanker, handling hose pipes to dampen the flames, etc. before the fire got too close to the cargo of fuel, which would blow the whole ship – and the Barfleur to Kingdom Come. It was obvious to the Admiral that, if they were going to save the cargo of oil, something better must be done to shore up the port side of the tanker. They needed to get her, and her precious cargo, to Malta at all cost.

The Bermuda Star was now engaged in securing alongside the tanker, and with great difficulty, had to secure both ships in a near upright position. This had to be achieved by lying alongside the ship on the port side, to heave the heavy tanker into – as near as possible – an upright position. An almost impossible situation, given the size of both ships, against the size of the stricken tanker, However, Barfleur had achieved it on the starboard side, SO??

"Who is the next senior ship in the squadron?" asked the Admiral turning to Trail.

"It must be Defender sir."

"Who is the Captain?

"Commander Cochran, he is a friend of mine, we came through Dartmouth together."

"In that case you inform him yourself that he is to take command of the remaining Fleet and proceed at best maximum speed to Malta, keeping me informed of any further casualties from enemy aircraft."

"Roger sir."

"And before you ask – yes, we will be shoring up Orion on her Port Side. Well? Jump to it Captain", the Admiral said with a wicked smile?

Trail smiled back and went off to carry out the Admiral's orders.

During the next ten hours or so, the whole ship's company was involved in securing the Bermuda star alongside the tanker and trying to relieve some of the pressure aboard HMS Barfleur It was indeed a mammoth task, but they finally got the two ships secured, one either side of the huge

Tanker. They began to make way, slowly at about six knots, at first, but, none the less – underway. There was a long way to go before they could get to Malta's Grand Harbour? HMS Defender had now taken control of the rest of the ships – or those that were left of the fleet.

They were now in some sort of order and sailing ahead in the more tranquil Mediterranean Sea. The fleet had suffered a loss of a number of the slower ships during the air attack, plus, one of the Frigates, trying to protect them, and pick up survivors. It had been an agonising experience for both Trail and the Admiral, who feltsomewhat helpless at times.

Suddenly a call came from the wireless office for Commander Trail.

"Aircraft approaching – range 10 miles."Trail rushed from the bridge to the radio room, and within minutes he called the bridge.

"Bridge, Radio room – aircraft approaching friendly – will shadow us home to Malta."

"Bridge, Roger – inform Barfleur we have made contact with friendly A|C."

"Radio room – Roger – message passed."

Trail returned to the bridge, where the Admiral and the helmsman were both standing side by side, and both were smiling – with relief it seemed?

"I think we handled that quite well Mr. Watts – don't you?

"Indeed we did Admiral," said the helmsman.

"I will relieve you now Sir," said Trail to the Admiral.

"And find a relief for Mr. Watts please Frank."

"No need Commander," said Watts "The watch will be changed at the normal time."

"And what would be the normal time Mr. Watts?

"The change – over is every two hours sir," he said.

"And how long have you been at the wheel?

"Can't quite recall at the moment Sir" Watts replied.

"Well, both You and the Admiral have been – "At The Wheel" – for the last eight, almost nine hours.

So I think a relief is in order. Don't you Admiral?

"Well it doesn't seem like eight and a half hours to me," said the Admiral "What say you, Mr. Watts?"

"Seems more like 24Hrs, or would be if I hadn't had an Admiral as my runner" Watts said, with a sideward glance at the Admiral.

Then all three men broke into hysterical laughter with relief.

It was at that very moment the Captain entered the Bridge. He stood staring at the three men but said nothing. The Admiral was the first to regain his composure.

"Ah! Captain" he said "Will you accompany me to your stateroom please, along with Commander Trail?

"Mr. Watts – your diligence and expertise in handling the ship under extreme conditions has been outstanding. I thank you, Sir."

With that, he turned to the Captain and said very politely "Captain Royce – If you please sir" He pointed the way to Royce. Who in turn said nothing at all but led the way to his stateroom.

The three ships were now secured together and slowly increasing speed, which had reached upwards of twelve knots, with the power of three ships engines and in a very calm sea. For the first time in a long time it seemed, The fleet, under the command of HMS Cavalier, were now well underway towards Malta, and ahead of the stricken ship by about forty or so miles. It was expected this part of the convoy would be tying up in Malta's Grand Harbour much earlier than expected; it was now around about 1730.

Suddenly the unmistakable sound of aircraft was heard. An immediate message was sent to HMS Barfleur warning of a possible attack. The three ships were alerted and went to action stations, and a sudden gloom was felt by all at the thought they had to avoid more attacks from the enemy.

"Bridge radio room. Friendly aircraft returning to relieve last escort" Another rousing cheer went up from the three ships. As night fell, the crews of the three ships began to relax and catch up on meals – which no-one had been able to savour for around about, twenty-four hours. The chef's onboard all three ships had been closed up at action stations alongside the rest of the crews, and they were all tired. However, they all got on with their "Day Jobs" to produce a meal, after which they could get some sleep before the next possible attack from the enemy. Fortunately, no such attack took place.

Defender, who had gone ahead with the other ships in convoy, reported their safe arrival at Grand Harbour at about 09:30 The tanker plus escort, was picked up on radar at about 13:00, some 20 miles away, ETA at Grand harbour, Malta, approximately 15:00 was the message received by radio.

Great rejoicing had already begun ashore, the seven surviving merchant ships and four remaining warships arrived safely at Grand Harbour. Plus, the whole population of Malta, it seemed, had turned out to welcome the remaining three ships, who would undoubtedly receive a similar reception on arrival.

The Bermuda Star, The Barfleur, and the Tanker came into view at 14:05 and slowly made way through the harbour entrance by 15:00, as forecast. This was a tricky manoeuvre, with the three ships getting through the entrance as one. It was achieved with great skill and seamanship, and they sailed into Grand Harbour, to a huge reception of cheering and flag-waving. It seemed like the whole of the Maltese population had turned out to greet the heroes of the moment, and a huge sigh of relief went up from the crew of the three vessels, along with cheering and cap waving.

The task of disengaging the Barfleur and the Bermuda Star from alongside the Tanker was tricky. It took four tugs expertly easing themselves between the two supporting vessels, and the tanker, two each side of the bows and two each side at the stern. It seemed to be a simple operation for these Tug men, and it was completed in less than an hour, as opposed to some nine or ten hours to get Bermuda Star alongside the huge Tanker when they were at sea.

On completion, of the transfer, the Bermuda Star made for an anchorage on the other side of the harbour, and, again it seemed, every dockyard worker on the Island swarmed aboard, and the job of unloading the cargo they had carried from the docks in Southampton began. This included the all the Naval armament loaded at the start of the voyage.

Before the Admiral and Commander Trail disembarked, and while the four tugs were carrying out their disengaging manoeuvres, the Admiral mustered all the ships company and the Naval team on deck to address the crew.

"Gentlemen" he began, "It has been an honour to have served with you during this dangerous, hazardous, but nonetheless successful voyage. You have been a credit to our Merchant Fleet, and a Godsend to the people of Malta. May the rest of your journey, be it East or West, be successful. Thank you, and God Speed."

At the conclusion of the Admiral's Speech, The Chief Engineer stepped forward.

"Gentlemen, I'm sure that you will all join with me when I say, that we have all learned something exceptional from this journey, our thanks must go to the Royal Navy for their expertise in gun handling, and the teaching of our – now expert gunners? A slight cheer rang out from those who had learned their gun handling expertise from their Naval colleagues. I would also like to thank the Admiral, in particular, and his Mate – (looking at helmsman Watts) for steering the ship through hazardous experiences whilst under fire, and of course Commander Trail, for his expertise running the ship in the absence of the Captain, who was indisposed."

Commander Trail raised his eyebrows at this last statement, but he did appreciate why the Chief Engineer said what he did. The Captain had already gone ashore. He went when the four tugs had disengaged the two ships from the Tanker's side. No one saw him go.

"Thank you again Admiral and Commander Trail, and of course the gunners." He looked across at the Petty Officer and the (now) six ratings, smiled and said, "We must not forget our guns crew's, both RN and civilian, who showed a shining, example of courage and fortitude under extreme conditions, as did you all."

Commander Trail now stepped forward.

"Thank you, chief. The Admiral and I will be disembarking shortly. We will be leaving four of our gunners behind to assist you in dismantling the armoury you have; the Admiral has also decided to leave behind two of the bridge wing automatic guns, plus ammunition, for your own Gunners, to give you some support in your onward journey. Thank you again, gentlemen, and may good luck follow you all the way to Suez, your next destination." With that, both officers disembarked on a waiting Naval boat, and headed toward the jetty at Valletta, to be greeted by the outgoing Admiral.

Back on Bermuda Star the Chief Officer, Phillip Rogers, turned to the ship's Company.

"Gentlemen, you were not meant to be informed yet, of our onward journey, but now you know. However, we will be here in Malta for at least two weeks, during which time we will disembark the goods and equipment we have carried from Southampton, we will also carry out a full paint job. (Grown, from crew)! Don't worry, most of the painting will be carried out by the Maltese Dockers" A huge sigh of relief went up from the assembled crew members.

"In the meantime, until the Captain returns, I suggest you all get some rest. This has been, probably – one of the most dangerous voyages we have encountered on this ship. You have all reacted with tremendous courage and fortitude which, I promise, will not be held back from the Company. Now gentlemen carry on please."

A slight cheer went up from the crew as they dismissed to their respective messes. The day went on, not as normal, but as usual. The crew had been laid off for rest, there were still things that had to continue – not least of all, the two chefs – who had been left to get on with, as slap up a meal as was possible – under the circumstances – with the ship swarming with people (Civilian dock workers ETC) unloading everything that had been brought in from the British Isles.

About 15.30h the Captain arrived back onboard. The quartermaster was on the blind side of the ship to where the Captain boarded, so obviously he was unseen by the quartermaster, who was, in fact, assisting the dockyard workmen in their loading of the equipment and stores into the barges alongside the ship. The Captain went unseen to his cabin and locked the door on entry. He poured himself a large glass of scotch, which of course was most unusual for this man in particular, a devout Christian who had not been known to drink alcohol. He downed his drink, undressed and went to his bunk. He fell asleep as soon as his head hit the pillow.

During the Captain's absence from his ship, frantic searching was going on both onboard and ashore. His cabin door was locked, and there was no response to the door knocking, so it was assumed that he had gone to visit friends on the Island, to satisfy himself that they were alive after the tremendous bombing that had been taking place on Malta. The Chief Steward, who knew that the Captain had close friends on the Island, made the assumption that this was so, and since his friends were all devout church-men, it seemed to be the obvious answer. "The Captain will no doubt stay ashore tonight, so I will worry about it tomorrow. Hopefully, it will ease his frame of mind. He did need a rest."? So said Mr. Summers.

During the next 24 hours, the ship was being relieved of the cargo she had carried from Southampton. The crew were assisting as required, but the Maltese workers had taken over the de-storing and were experts at the job. The Chief Officer ordered the ship's crew to let the Maltese Dockers get on with it, and the crew to get on with cleaning the upper deck where possible, and to assist the Maltese Dockers, but only if they asked for help. It took the best part of three days before the cargo was finally discharged from the hold, and a further day to off-load the RN armament. During all this activity, no one had even thought of the Captain's absence. The Chief Officer assumed that he was still ashore, and had decided to remain with his Christian friends until the ship was rid of the cargo. It had been five days since he was last seen on board the ship.

On the last day of unloading, the crew turned to with a will, to clean and re-assemble the upper deck and begin repainting. There was a heavy task ahead of them in the following week, to get the ship cleaned and painted before they could sail again on to their next port of call, which was presumably Suez. Dave Summers, having not looked for the Captain since his disappearance, began his own rounds now, which was not only the necessary storage of food etc. for the forthcoming trip East, but also the cleanliness of his own department. That included the Captain's cabin, which he had not visited since the Captain had gone ashore.

He set to, and went to the cabin with his own keys, inserted the key in the lock, and found he could not get past an obstruction. He must be back Summers thought and knocked the door. There was no answer, Summers then knocked harder on the door and shouted, "Captain this is the chief steward are you there, please open the door so that I can see to your cabin."

Summers was expecting to hear a reply; maybe the Captain was using his own toilet or his own shower facility and didn't hear him. He decided to give him another ten minutes or so before he came back. He left the cabin and went back to the wardroom. A few of the ship's officers were taking a short break for coffee etc. "Anybody see the Captain return on board this morning'? he asked They all said that they hadn't seen him at all since they assumed he was ashore.

Summers turned around and went straight back to the Captain's cabin and tried the Key in the door again, this time, it did open, and the steward went in. The cabin was a mess like it had not been cleaned for a long time, Clothes, charts and navigational aids were strewn all over the cabin, there were also two empty whiskey bottles several beer bottles and glasses. The Captain was sitting in his armchair in a filthy state, and in his underwear, he was unshaven with about a week's growth of beard and seemed to be in a trance. Dave Summers had been a ship's steward for many years, but even he was set back by the state of the Captain.

He went over to him in the chair put his hand on his shoulder and shook him gently—

"Captain, this is the Chief Steward, are you awake? Royce opened his eyes with a start.

"Ah my chief steward, Mr. Summers" He spoke with a slur as if he were drunk.'

"Captain," said Summers "Are you OK? Where have you been, I thought you were ashore with your friends, I have been concerned about you."

Summers looked about the room, and it was obvious the Captain had been drinking – heavily, a very unusual situation. He was a teetotaller moreover. There had never been so much as a bottle of lemonade in the Captain's cabin in all the years the steward had known him. Dave Summers was frankly, astounded. However, he must not let any of the crew know. "Captain I'm going to get you some food, try to relax until I return. No one else will know of this except the Chief Engineer. Do not attempt to go out of this cabin; I'll be back very shortly, do you understand me, Captain?"

"Yes, I understand," he said, with a slur.

"OK I am going to lock the door, so do not attempt to come out of your cabin," he said, "I will be back very shortly" Summers locked the cabin door, and immediately sought out the chief engineer, who luckily happened to be in the wardroom.

"Mr. Evans, could I speak with you a minute please sir."

"Yes, of course, Mr. Summers – how can I help?

Summers called the engineer over to a corner out of earshot but asked him briefly to accompany him outside. Summers conducted the engineer out onto the upper deck and went up forward to the bow before he explained the Captain's condition.

"Good God" exclaimed Evans "Has he been on board all the time we have been unloading?"

"I'm not sure, but by the state of him, I think he must have. I know for sure he hasn't had anything to eat, but he's seen off a couple of bottles of whiskey by the look of things."

"Whiskey? I've never known him to drink in all the years I've known him, come on, let's go and see what he's been up to."

When they entered the Captain's cabin, Royce was still in the same position as he was when the steward left the room. When he saw the Chief Engineer, he broke down and started to cry; both officers looked at each other in amazed embarrassment.

"Captain, pull yourself together man," said the Chief Engineer "what on earth have you been up to these last five days? We assumed you were ashore with your Christian friends and decided to leave us to it, which was why no one tried to contact you. Taff Summers had never heard his friend Rowland Evans lose his cool before, but he certainly cut no slack with the Captain as he told him in no uncertain way,

"You will move into My cabin immediately until we get your own accommodation sorted out. You will shower, eat a meal – in my cabin. Your uniform will be there for you to dress – like a Captain – and you will present yourself to the crew at quarters, first thing in the morning. Are you clear about that Captain? No one else in this ship will know anything about this Pathetic episode. I will write a speech for you to read out to the Ships Company. Taff: here is my door key, make sure the coast is clear then give me a hand with him."

The Chief Steward looked out into the passageway and opened the door to the Chief engineer's room, which was immediately opposite the Captain's room, he got hold of the Captain under the arm, as did Evans.

"All clear Rowland", said Summers and they both heaved the Captain across the passage and into the opposite cabin. They sat the Captain in Evans's only chair, a comfortable armchair, and his favourite. The engineer's cabin was not quite as large as the Captain's room, but it would have to do for the moment. It was Rowland's only retreat, and he did not like the thought of the Captain in his private domain, but needs must when the devil drives, (as the saying goes!). The Chief engineer said "I'm not going to sit here with him," he nodded at the Captain. "Is there anyone we can trust to keep his mouth shut about this Taff?"

"Yes, one of my boys. I'll go and get him."

"Well hurry up I've got an engine to work on," he said. "And get his cabin cleaned up so we can put him back in his own bunk. I don't want my cabin stinking of whiskey or ruddy gin, whatever he's been drinking all the week. As soon as he is sober make him eat something."

"OK Chief," said the steward, and sped off to get one of his team to babysit the Captain.

The steward had never seen the chief engineer lose his cool before, in all the years he had known him, this time, however!? Summers found his second steward, the man in whom he could trust to keep his mouth shut. When they returned to the engineer's cabin, it appeared the Captain had gone to sleep in the engineer's chair again.

"I'll leave you to it Taff, let me know the state of things later. I'll want my cabin back as soon as he is awake, and get this brewery Detoxified ok?

"Of course Chief – I can trust my steward."

With that, the engineer left them to it.

"Now then Geordie," said the chief steward " you know what I want you to do, so get over to the Old man's cabin and clean it up – spotless. I'm sorry I can't give you anybody to help, but we have to keep his – (nodded towards the sleeping Captain) – nibs a secret, you understand of course that's why I chose you. I won't tell you just now; I'll put you right afterwards. This cabin is like a Tip, I'm sorry about that, but I can't give you any help for obvious reasons, but just Do your job, keep your Gob shut, which I know you will, and reap the benefit?"

"OK, Boss, I know the drill, and you can count on me."

"I know I can count on you George – especially if you want your Head Stewards post?? Summers laughed jokingly, knowing he could count on his senior steward.

"Gercha, you Welshmen are all alike" he also laughingly retorted.

Summers left the Captain's cabin and went to the ward-room where most of the ships' Officers were relaxing prior to lunch. Summers was also the head man in charge of any alcohol the officers may want. It was usual for anyone to have a drink with lunch whilst in harbour, and the steward asked – "anyone for the bar?"

"Yes please Taff," said one or two of the officers.

"Please help yourselves, gentlemen, the tick board is in the right-hand corner." Everyone's name was on the board, they ticked their names as required, and their bar bill was paid for at the end of each month. No one had used the bar very much before they reached Malta because no one had a lot of time to relax of late, most officers had been working in their departments since they had arrived. Now they were all squared away and ready to sail. They knew they were going to Suez for fuel, and then on into the Indian Ocean, but no one knew their final destination, and why all the way to Suez before they could refuel?

Rowland Evans came into the wardroom for lunch, "Morning gentlemen" he said, "before we sit down to lunch, I have some news about our departure. We will sail tomorrow about 1100, most of you will assume we are heading for the Suez Canal, and you will be correct, I don't quite understand why we have to fuel in Suez, especially now that Malta has been replenished. I assume it was all organised beforehand. The Chief Steward and I, have been ashore to organise a top up for the larder. No one is positive about our movements at the moment; we could end up in Ceylon for all I know! But we are getting victuals supplied to us by the good old RN supply depot. It could be we will head South down the African coast, or maybe carry on East into the Indian Ocean. Whatever the situation is, the Captain will be advising us first thing in the morning. He is now back on board and busy with charts and planning the route etc. this will not concern anyone at the moment, suffice to say we will assemble the whole ship's company at 09:30h tomorrow morning, be advised everyone is required to be there. I have to tell you Gentlemen, this next leg of our journey could be a long one, especially if we go East, we will find that out in the morning. You should have as relaxing an evening as you dare, but I want no hangovers OK? Now then let's have lunch, you may also have drinks with lunch if you would like."

It was the senior officers prerogative to allow the officers to use the bar on a workday. Surprisingly the only taker was the junior radioman, who put his glass back as soon as he realised he was alone at the bar? At the end of lunch, most of the officers sat around in their comfortable wardroom and had coffee and a relaxing chat, something none of them had been able to do for some time.

At about two thirty in the afternoon, George, the chief steward's man, sought out his boss in the wardroom pantry, not in front of the other officers, to tell him that he had cleaned the Captain's cabin, and if he wanted to re-house the Captain it was OK to do so now. Summers sought out the chief engineer and suggested they both go to his cabin and shift the Captain back into his own room.

"Gladly, said Evans, "and get someone to fumigate my cabin, will you, it's probably smelling like a brewery by now – let's go."

They went first into the Captain's cabin to check out that it was satisfactory, the Geordie Steward had done an excellent job, and they proceeded to re-house the drunken Captain. On entering the engineer's cabin, they found everything was in order, the Captain was awake and had either got Taff's steward to do it, or he had cleaned the engineer's cabin himself. As they entered, the Captain was just adjusting the engineer's seat.

"Ah! Chief Engineer and Mr. Summers, thank you chief for the use of your cabin, I have had it cleaned for you. It seemed to have been in a mess.! I will be in my cabin, probably for the remainder of the day. I have chart work to do. Will you ask my First Officer, Mr. Rogers to come to my cabin?" With that, he pushed past the two officers and went to his own cabin across the passageway. Both Evans and Summers looked at each other in absolute amazement, then burst out into hysterical laughter.

"Come on Taff, let's get out of this madhouse – I don't believe it," he said shaking his head.

The following morning at the appointed 09:30, the ship's company had assembled on the foredeck to be talked to by the Captain. He appeared before his Ships Company, smartly dressed in his number one uniform.

"Gentlemen, he began. It has been my honour to have served with you aboard this ship The Bermuda Star, for these past seven years. We will be sailing for the Suez Canal today at approximately 13:00h. Lunch will be early at 11:30h, and I expect every department's senior officer to be available when I inspect: – each area, personally, beginning at 12:00. Any delay to my inspections, which may delay the ship's sailing time, will be noted in the Ship's log, and the perpetrator of the delay will incur a fine of not less than £100. That is all. First Officer Rogers. Dismiss the men."

With that, Royce turned and walked away toward the bridge with Officers, and the whole crew looking agog at the Captain's departure. The first officer moved towards the front, but he was stopped by the chief engineer.

"Hold on Philip," he said quietly and confronted the astounded ships company.

"Gentlemen," he said "At this stage, I would ask you to ignore the last statement by the Captain. I'm sure that his I'll health is affecting his judgement. I will ask you to dismiss and go about your business. It is likely that an inspection will take place, but rest assured we will sail at the appropriate time. Dismiss to your parts of the ship." He turned to the ship's officers and said: "Please adjourn to the wardroom gentlemen."

The Engineer led the way, followed by the rest of the officers. When they all sat down in the wardroom, the steward asked his sidekick to get an urn of tea going. The chief officer again confronted the assembled officers.

"Well I don't know what to say at this stage, but I am sure that you will understand the Captain is not himself, I don't know if he would see a medic even if I sent for one. It is far too late in the day before we sail and it will be too late for me to go ashore and try to get through to the company. I will go ashore if it is necessary, but I don't want to delay sailing. I don't even know what the sailing orders are; he has not confided in me at all since we reached Malta, or before we left the UK come to that, I worked that out myself."

"Damnit I will go ashore," he suddenly said.

"Phillip, you will come with me, you are The First Officer, and I am the Senior person on board, Senior to the Captain even. Chief Steward, see if you can calm him down till I get back. I don't know what I will achieve, but here goes.

Philip, you haven't pulled the ship's boat inboard yet have you?

"I don't think so chief, let's go see if it is. I'll put her back in the water." The motor boat had not been pulled inboard, so the Chief Officer seconded a seaman to drive the boat inboard to Grand harbour landing steps, where both officers jumped off and headed for the shipmasters office.

Evans produced his ships officers identification pass, as did Rogers, and asked how they might get hold of Commander Trail, who disembarked with the Admiral two weeks ago. It was a bit of long shot, but their luck was in.

"I know Commander Trail Sir," he said "Wait one minute, and I will see if I can get him."

Within a few minutes, the young sailor gave him the phone.

"Hello, who is speaking please?"

"Oh, hello is this Commander Trail? This is Chief Engineer Evans of Bermuda Star here. Is it possible I could meet with you in person Commander, I have a very urgent demand to make which could delay our sailing to Suez"?

"Yes certainly chief, are you at the grand harbour landing?

"Yes I am Sir."

"I'll send someone to get you, be there in about five minutes."

"Thank you, Sir, very kind of you."

True to his word, the transport arrived, it was a blue navy van, driven by a pretty wren in a white uniform, who whisked them away to commander Trail's Office. On arrival, Frank Trail met them in person.

"How nice to see you again Mr. Evans, and you too Phillip – How can I be of assistance?

"Well, I'm not sure how to start here Commander."

"Frank, please Chief," said Trail in his usual pleasant self.

"I have a serious problem Frank, and I need some advice. As you will remember, no doubt, you spent a lot of time trying to find a missing Captain while we were under attack at sea, and on several occasions on our voyage to Gibraltar, and then at sea again on our way to Malta. Nobody knows to this day where he was when we were under enemy attack."

Evans went on to explain all that had happened onboard in the past two and a half weeks, and finishing with today's outburst from the Captain.

"Is he that unstable Rowland?" asked Trail.

"I'm afraid so Frank. The more I consider it, the more I believe he is in no fit state to continue with this voyage, or be in command of this ship come to that. I worry that he could be a danger to the crew if under attack by the enemy on – what is to me – an unknown destination at the moment, due to the Captain's state of mind."

Trail turned to Phillip Rogers.

"What do you think Phillip could he command the ship in a crisis?"

"I have to agree with Roland, Frank.

The Captain's recent actions have been most unusual, especially the disappearances when we were under attack, where did he go? That is the most perplexing situation of all, we even looked in the forward bilge, out of desperation. He was never the easiest person to engage with, but I have never seen him like this before. He did, however, have a meeting in London with the owners while you away Roland. I didn't mention it to you when you came back because I didn't think it relevant. He always saw the owners at some stage before we sailed, and I thought it the Norm."

"Well he has never confided in me, and I am, after all the Chief Engineer," said Evans. "He has never confided in me about anything, what our destinations will be, not our port of call, what our pick up cargo is to be, or even if there is a pickup cargo. It is all very confusing. But with him, it was, as Philip said, The norm.

I have no way of contacting the company for advice on the future of the Voyage, I have never been informed of where we are going. He turned to Philip Rogers and asked: "Did he ever say anything to you about our departure or our destination Phil?"

"The only indication I had of forthcoming sailings were,

that we would be taking part In a very important voyage in the very near future. He sent for me again that day. It was the day after you had left for home Roland, he informed me of the loading of stores, and ammunition, etc. I had no idea what it was until the dockyard started loading everything on board, then I took it for granted that we were going somewhere? But where? I was not informed until we sailed for Devonport and joined up with the fleet."

Evans then said, "Each time I have approached the subject of our destination I have been fobbed off with a story from him that is beyond belief. He would say" "I am unable to pass on our final destination, not even to you chief. When I am at liberty to do so, you will be informed."

"This has been his answer every time I have approached the subject. under these circumstances, – the like-of which, I have never known before in all my years at sea as an engineer. I am now wondering if it is safe for him to hold command of the ship, in his present state of mind, and the possibility of having to defend the ship against attack, etc. I really am stuck for an answer, and I fear that if we were to encounter an enemy attack be it a ship, aircraft or even perhaps a submarine, there would be no way of telling what his reaction would be, especially for the safety of a civilian crew?"

Frank Trail had been listening intently to the chief engineer's concerns, especially the safety of the crew comments he made.

"You say, Roland, that as Senior Chief Engineer, and the eldest officer on the ship, you knew nothing about your true destination?" "No. When I returned on board from Wales, after my wife's funeral, I had been away from the ship for four days. It was quite late when I got back, about, 22:00h I think. I went to see the Captain before I got changed into my engine room kit, he was, as usual – full of his own self-importance. He knew why I'd been home, but couldn't help himself making a comment about the time I had taken to return. I wasn't about to cause any more unpleasantness; I was not in any mood for explanations, so I just left. I got changed and went straight to the engine room. The rest of his antics you encountered yourself while you were on board."

"Roland," said Trail "I can't believe what I'm hearing here. I can obviously see the predicament you, and Philip are in, what is it that you think I can help you with?"

"Well Frank, as you see, I have no contact with the Ship Owners and I was hoping that – perhaps you could, maybe, through your communications systems, find out for me – who are the owners of the Bermuda Star? Pass on the information to me, and I can see if I can contact them personally, to get the information I need to continue with the voyage. "I'm sure we can do that Roland," Trail said,

"But what is your intent now. Do you intend to sail under his orders, or will you wait for any information I can get? It may take a little time, or it may take a long time before I can give you any answers, and during the lull, I should think you will be expected to get the ship underway."

"I intend to delay as long as possible with a sudden problem in the engine room, but he may not fall for that one, it's too much like an old stokers trick."

"The trouble is Roland, how will I get the information to you if you have already sailed"?

"I've thought about that too Frank. Normally we will have the radio manned on a four hourly check-in system, you probably have our call sign, you used it often enough when you were on board. I'll keep an operator on full time, as opposed to our current four hourly checks. The old man won't like it, but I'll convince him that we need to know what enemy aircraft are in the area we will be sailing in, you never know, luck might be on our side, and he will see the sense in it."

"Well, I'll certainly do what I can this end. But I can't believe you are in such a predicament Roland, and I'm sure you Philip, have an even tougher job on your hands under these conditions, I'm on your side, and I'll be in touch, rest assured."

"Thank you so much, Frank. I'll carry on as the ignorant stoker he thinks I am" said Roland.

The two officers left commander Trail and returned to the ship, this time by a local civilian boat which was very much like a gondola.

Back on board the two officers went straight to the wardroom, where they were greeted by most of the officers who had finished lunch, and were waiting for the Captain's, so-called inspection.

It was now 12:45h and no inspection had taken place. The Chief Steward had put lunches aside for the two officers and invited them to sit down and eat before anything took place with the Captain's inspection. The Engineer declined the offer.

"I need to go and check a few things before we sail, thanks, Taff, I'll have a cup of tea though, I'm as dry as a bone" He had his cup of tea, gulping it down in a hurry.

"I'll fill you in when I come back Phillip," he said to the First officer and went out of the wardroom.

Evans went straight to the Captain's cabin and knocked the door; there was no reply, so he tried the door handle, it was locked. He then went to the bridge; the Captain was not there either. Damn it he said to himself; he's gone again He checked with the quartermaster at the gangway, he said he thought he had seen the Captain going for'ard towards the hatch ladder for the hold where they stowed cargo.

"Thanks, Harry," said Evans and proceeded to the hatch for the hold. He noticed the hatch tarpaulin had been pulled back from the hatch cover, and he wondered who in hell was down there. He put his hand on the hatch lid handle and pulled to lift. It was locked. He assumed someone had forgotten to throw the tarpaulin back where it should have been or was still waiting for the Captain's inspection to take place. He adjusted that and tied it back to the cleats on the side of the hatch cover. This tarpaulin cover prevented water, especially sea water in heavy weather, crashing onto the hatch and getting onto cargo, etc. I wonder who left that, he thought, although it could have been left like that for the Captain's inspection. He left it secured again now anyway, and proceeded to the anchor deck to check everything was in order before the Captain found anything else he could pick on, and give the deck hands a bit more grief before they sailed. He went back to the bridge where Mr. Watts, as he was now known to the whole ship's crew, since his "Friend" the Admiral commended him when he left the ship.

"Ah Tom, he said have you seen the Captain anywhere?

"Well now, it's a funny thing Chief but I thought I saw him going down the forward hatch to the hold a while back. Part of his inspection I supposed, but I've seen him do that before, never took too much notice of it though. You know what he's like."

"When did you see him do that before Tom?"

"It was while I was on watch, during the outward trip from Plymouth, when they put that heavy gun on top of the hatch, I saw him directing the Navy to leave the hatch cover clear, or at least that's what it looked like to me."

"Thanks, Tom, keep your eyes pinned will you, and if you see him go down again let me know as soon as you see it. Discreetly of course.

This is very important Tom, and I want you to keep your eyes pinned and contact me immediately if you see him either enter or leave the forward hatch and at what time."

"Ok Chief, I'll keep my eye open from now on then."

Evans left the bridge and went to find Philip Rogers and the Chief Steward. As it happened, they were both in the wardroom, still awaiting the Captain's inspection. He entered the wardroom, and all the Officers looked up to find out what was happening.

"Gentlemen, I don't think we will bother about the Captain's so called rounds at the moment. Please return to your compartments and carry on as normal. I'm not sure yet what our sailing orders are, but I will get to that eventually. No questions at the moment, suffice to say that we may not sail today due to problems?"

Everyone but the Engineer, the First Officer and the Chief Steward left the wardroom, all of them confused and angry at the Captain's disappearance again. It was obvious that something was amiss, and annoying, for everyone. But to be treated in a manner that appeared to concern only the chief officer, the chief engineer and the steward, was not acceptable. Everyone should have been put in the picture.

When the wardroom was empty of the other officers, Evans turned to the First Officer and the steward.

"We have a real problem," he said "Phillip I would like you to try and contact Commander Trail.

Ask him if he has found anything out about Royce,

explain to him that we think he may be passing on information to the enemy about ship movements within the fleet. He put his hands up to calm the two officers. "Hang on, and I'll explain. During our trip down from Plymouth, he kept disappearing, Remember? He was hunted for, everywhere, except in the hold: correct? Even Commander Trail scouted around for him to no avail, when we were at sea, and under fire. Next . . . He disappeared ashore on quite a few occasions before we left Southampton, while I was away for four days, you mentioned that to me, Phillip, believing he went to London for two days, no one has checked, nor should they of course, but the question remains: DID he go to London or did he go elsewhere, and if elsewhere – where?

"Hang on boss," Taff said "your beginning to sound like a Policeman."

"That's as maybe Taff, but something isn't right you must agree.

What are your thoughts, Phillip?

"Certainly something is amiss chief I agree. Yes, I'll try and contact Frank Trail, he may have received some information by now, I'll get on to it at once."

"OK Phillip, thanks, I must go and have a word with Heads of departments. They probably think I'm the wicked witch of the Mediterranean by now. I'll see you when you come back. Taff, you come with me, and we will explain to everyone in the wardroom."

"Right Boss, I'll assemble the Officers in the wardroom again." The steward went off to inform the ship's Officers, He did not want to call them on the loudspeaker in case it was heard by the Captain, but no one knew where he was, so it might not matter, however, to be on the safe side?

As it happened, most of the ships officers were already

back in the wardroom, when the three had left. They were very upset by the engineer's dismissal, which most of them had thought was very unfair and intended to make the point. Just at that moment, Roland Evans came back into the wardroom as well.

"Thank you, gentlemen. I must firstly apologise for my seeming rudeness when we dispersed; it was not meant to be a dismissal like that. I was in a real predicament not knowing what was going on with our departure from Malta. We are all in a bit of a pickle under the circumstances I think, please accept my sincere apologies for my rudeness. That is not like me, but nonetheless, I was out of line This has been about the most frustrating two weeks I have ever had on board this ship, probably on any ship I should think. However, the First Officer has gone ashore to speak to the Navy again about our departure, and, hopefully, confirm our destination from the ship's owners – if they can be traced. I personally have not spoken to any of the company management since I accepted this appointment about four years ago. This trip was also meant to be my last voyage before I retire. It may seem like an unorthodox method, but in view of the Captain's state of mind, I'm trying to confirm from the owners of Bermuda Star, the true destination of our next port of call, and to confirm if Captain Royce is fit to command? In my opinion, he is not fit, and too ill to undertake this next stage of our voyage. We have all assumed that we are going to another destination after Malta. But there is nothing to confirm what the next cargo is that we must load, or where our next port of call will be to load a cargo, and of course, where we should be going to disembark that cargo. I am hoping that First Officer Rogers will bring us some good news on his return. Until then we must make a bigger effort to find

Captain Royce.I want to find the Captain safe, somewhere on board. I want the cargo hold opened up as if to load a new cargo. Every inch to be inspected, and though we don't carry them usually? I want no stone unturned! The Captain MUST be somewhere on board. Find Him!"

The whole wardroom rose as one and left to go and seek out the Captain's whereabouts, assuming he was on board of course.

After several hours of continuous searching, including; lifting the hatches and tarpaulin from the hold, there was still no sign of him. The whole ship had been inspected from stem to stern by everyone on board, except, of course, the chef's, who were hard at it in the galley. They still had stomachs to fill.

It was late into the evening before Philip Rogers returned on board. All the officers were assembled in the wardroom, having finished dinner. They were waiting for Phillip Rogers's return, for any information he had, about the Captain of course.

"Let me get you a drink Phillip said the steward, have you had anything to eat since you went ashore?

"Yes, thanks, Taff, I'm as dry as a bone, though, you can get me something long and cold please, and before I start let me catch my breath."

Roland Evans intervened and said, "Let's give the man a chance to get his breath please gentlemen. Taff have you still got the First Officer's dinner?

"No, that's really OK Roland thank you, I ate with Frank Trail in the wardroom ashore. But I am now going to give you all the biggest surprise you have ever had. In the first place, there is no Company Office anymore. In fact, there is no company."

"What!"

A gasp went up among the whole wardroom.

Rogers continued,

"It seems that the owners sold this ship, the last one of eight ships left in the company name, to a consortium called R.O.Y.C. Ltd. It also seems that the name of this ship – BERMUDA STAR – no longer exists. The ship's name was deleted from the company books when Royce bought it. It had been offered for scrap to another company, who turned it down, and it seems that Royce bought it, along with the contract to carry out this assignment with the Royal Navy. Royce retained the ship's name illegally, and he should have changed it before he took possession. It would seem that whoever agreed to the contract initially, possibly the Admiralty, had failed to correct the mistake, or had not noticed anything amiss since it all seems to have taken place very quickly, during a time when the allocation of cargo, in this case, desperately needed cargo for Malta had already been assigned, but there it is. Frank Trail is doing all he can to help us. The amount paid for the ship was believed to be £50,000:00. Captain Trail, was raised to the position of Captain RN. just after his arrival in Malta, and he Is, incidentally, looking into the situation for us now, and of course for the Navy, to ascertain if it was legal for this ship to have undertaken this assignment to Malta in the first place. Also in view of the risks to life of this ship's civilian crew, who had placed themselves under enemy fire, unbeknown to them at the outset, and they will be in further danger if the next assignment proceeds, to goodness knows where? There is also another BUT! It would seem that the R.O.Y.C. Ltd. Company has secured a contract from a Maltese Company, to proceed on to another port – unknown at this time – but it is believed to be in Mozambique, and I think I had better stop at this point. But like I said, the Royal Navy under Captain Trail are Investigating this area in Africa, which is believed to be under German control."

"No wonder it took you so long to get back Phillip, well done," said Evans. "But this now throws a whole new light on the subject of course. Gentlemen, we have a lot to ponder upon, to say the least. We will not disclose any of this information to the crew at this time, or they might all jump ship? Sorry gentlemen a poor joke. However, we must first of all find out where the Captain is? We will not be too worried about his welfare at the moment, but I want the whole crew's welfare to be protected, including of course wages, etc. This will be the first thing they will be thinking about, and so we should also. The Captain is not on board unless he is hiding in some cubbyhole somewhere. So It is possible he is ashore with the Maltese company he seems to be in business with, and we have no way of knowing who that company is at the moment. We will close this meeting for the time being. There is nothing we can change or do until we find out the Captain's whereabouts, which I suspect could be ashore with the new company – HIS new company – customers. I suggest we now all check our departments and ensure things are as they should be, and turn in. We must wait until the Captain returns on board. If he does return, that is. Goodnight gentlemen."

The Chief Engineer looked for the night watchman, who happened to be Mr. Watts, the Admirals best mate, "Evening Mr. Watts."

"Evening Chief, how can I help? He asked in his usual polite way."

"You and I have both known the Captain for a good few

years, at sea and ashore, you have been closer to him than many on board I should think. But this time, I can't make it out. He's disappeared again, ashore somewhere I, can't find him, When, and If, he returns on board during your watch, please don't hesitate to call me. I haven't seen him for a good few days, he might be with his Christian friends, I don't know, but I am anxious to see him about sailing. I'd be obliged."

"He came on board not twenty minutes ago chief, a bit tipsy if you ask me, sir?

"That's interesting George If you ask me – which you won't, of course," The engineer said with a wink.

"I hope he went to his cabin this time chief; I can't keep track on him these days."

"Thanks, George, keep an eye on him, if he attempts to go ashore again, you or your relief should call me immediately, I know you will keep it to yourself but I'm worried. He keeps disappearing and no one can find him. I wonder if he goes up the crow's nest? What do you think George? It's the only place we haven't looked for him.

"I shouldn't think so chief. He wouldn't know how to get back down – I know he can't fly – but then he is the Captain, so he knows more than me. Goodnight chief, I'll keep you up to date."

"Thanks, George – G'nite"

Mr. Evans went off to his cabin and turned in. He found he was very tired and went to sleep immediately.

Mr. Watts was carrying out his duties as night watchmen, patrolling around the decks from the bridge to the stern and then up to the anchor cable and returning to the bridge. As he left the cable deck, he thought he heard an unusual sound. He stopped at the bottom of the forepeak ladder, to listen again, but heard nothing more. He returned to the bridge and kept a keen eye on the anchor cable. Nobody could be up there surely, and it was unlikely anyone could be in the anchor cable fore-hatch? That was the area where the anchor cable was stowed when raised from or dropped off the ship to lay the anchor on the seabed. He thought of calling the chief engineer but then thought better of it. He would tell the chief in the morning what he thought he had heard.

Watts finished his duty as watchkeeper at 06:00, being relieved by the next on watch. He didn't bother to say anything about the peculiar noise he thought he heard, He turned over his watch. It was past early dawn, and the sun was low on the horizon. George Watts was not a man who would let something like a noise on watch worry him, but before he went to his bunk, he walked up forward to the anchor cable stowage. He was about to check the cargo hold hatch, when a voice from the other side of ship called out to him in a loud voice.

"Mr. Watts, what are you doing messing with the tarpaulin of the hatch cover?

"Oh Captain, I didn't see you there, I thought I heard some flapping of the tarpaulin when I was on watch on the bridge, and like a good seaman I came to check. It seems to be OK, now, it must have been a gust of wind that caught the corner of the cover, look, it seems to be a little bit loose on the corner. No problem though Captain, I'll just tighten it up a little bit. Probably someone caught their foot in the loose rope yesterday when we were securing the hatch covers, after we finished yesterday's clean up. No problem now sir, I've seen to it and I'm off to get a cup of tea, I've finished my watch. Good morning to you Captain.

"Yes, good morning indeed Mr. Watts," said the Captain,

and walked towards the bridge on the opposite side of the hatch.

Watts was sure he heard him whistling quietly. No, it couldn't have been, he thought. Watts went off to his mess; the time was now about 06:40. Just in time for a nice cup of tea and whatever the chefs have for breakfast he thought, and off he went.

Watts could not go to the chief engineer's cabin because that cabin was opposite the Captain's, so he headed for the chief steward who he knew would be up and about. He cornered the chief steward as he was entering the wardroom.

"Could I have a quick word Mr. Summers please – it is very urgent."

"Certainly George, give me a minute to put this hot stuff down" On his return back to the quartermaster George asked him if they could talk somewhere Private.

"Yes come into the pantry," said Summers, as they entered the steward shut the door.

"Now then George how can I help?

"I suspect Mr. Evans has told you; he asked me to look out for anything odd with the Captain. So here goes . . .

George Watts went through the whole episode with the steward as to the Captain's strange behaviour when he came off watch, and encounters he noticed before. "One thing that I managed to do, was to avoid my relief seeing me go forward, so to all intents and purpose, I was probably the only one who saw him. So there it is. If Mr. Evans wants to see me, I'm going to have some breakfast."

"Right then George – bloody well done – Mr. Evans will want to see you, for sure, so no sneaking ashore OK?"

"Chance would be a fine thing! he said and went off to breakfast.

Dave Summers had to wait for the Chief Engineer, who was down in the engine room at the moment, so the information had to wait a while. Not for long, however!

The Chief Steward, acting on the information imparted to him by George Watts, had gone straight to the Captain's cabin with a full breakfast on a tray, knocked on the door and walked in to see the Captain sitting at the dining table awaiting his meal as he would have done at any time before.

"Good morning Mr. Summers, it is a fine morning indeed, don't you think?"

"Yes indeed Captain. Shall I pour your tea? Or would you like to wait until you have finished eating?"

"I'll do it myself thank you Mr. Summers. And would you please ask the Chief Engineer to see me as soon as he is free. Thank you."

"Certainly Captain."

With that, the chief steward returned to the wardroom.

The Chief Engineer walked into the wardroom for breakfast at ten past seven.

"Morning Taff, what's the news from the front?"

"Right, pin your ears back boss and listen to me. We are the last in the wardroom everyone else has eaten so that I can speak freely."

"Oh Oh! I smell trouble."

"You certainly do boss. The Captain is in his cabin eating his breakfast like a good boy, but more to the point he actually seems to be normal. I can't guarantee how long it will hold out, but he is speaking normally, politely even, all I can say is he seems to be human? He wants to see you ASAP in his cabin,."

"I want to see him also, and the sooner the better" Evans said,

"Hang on a minute Roland, no point in blowing off steam, If it's just going to be a bullfight we need to find out what's happening on his side if we're ever going to get to the bottom of this mess."

"Yes your right Taff I suppose, but we must have answers. No one knows if we are employees or ruddy galley slaves. People have lost their lives sailing here to Malta. This ship has been lucky so far, but who knows if we will be lucky when we sail on to goodness knows where. I'll go and see our illustrious Captain right now, and you're coming with me."

Chief engineer Evans and Chief Steward Summers set out together for the Captain's cabin, determined to find out what was going on.

On arrival at Royce's cabin, they stormed in without knocking, to be greeted by the Captain, smiling, and with an open hand to shake. Neither of the officers acknowledged the offer.

"Please sit down Gentlemen, we have a lot to discuss."

At that moment there was another knock at the door, and in walked Phillip Rogers the First Officer. He also ignored the outstretched hand from the Captain as they all took a seat at the table.

"Now then, where do we start Gentlemen?"

"We start right here." Said a very irate engineer. We three SENIOR members of this ship's crew have been press-ganged into this illegal voyage under false pretenses. We also have young Cadets on this ship who, never having been to sea before in their lives, have unwittingly laid those young lives on the line, falsely believing they would be learning, eventually, to become Ship's Officers. a noble profession, worthy of praise for their courage during war. This also applies to the remainder of this crew both Officers and Men. This whole ship's company will be given an option when we assemble the whole crew, and I mean the WHOLE crew at 10:00. All of these men, Officers and Crew, will be given a full wage packet; plus, the option of going back home to Britain on the next ship leaving this island for their homeland."

Chief engineer Evans was laying down the law in his anger, not realising his anger would have no effect at all on what Royce could or could not do, but he continued.

"Now then Captain, it is your turn, to tell us three very senior officers, the whole truth about this voyage. And I mean the truth."

"Before I begin," said Royce,

"I must tell you that there is a bigger risk in leaving this ship than in remaining on board.

I will explain. Having worked for the company that owned this ship for seven years, I was well aware of the fact that it was owned by a very well respected, and prosperous company who, for many years, had lived in Warsaw. I don't know how many of you are aware that the owners of this ship were Jewish, and as you may know, during the nineteen thirty's, and leading up to the outset of war, the Jewish nation were ostracised by Hitler well before 1939, when the Germans marched into Poland. During that occupation, they killed over three million Jews and another three million Polish inhabitants. Such was Hitler's policy to rule the world, and wipe out the Jewish nation, amongst others. We now come to this Ship's present situation. I know it would appear that my actions of late have been – perhaps, Erratic? But I can assure you that my intentions were, honourable, but Secret under the circumstances. And Incidentally Chief, the transmitter you have been looking for is in the cable locker on the port side and in a strong steel box. It takes a bit of manoeuvring to get it ready to transmit.

You will now be wondering who I have been transmitting messages to. My youngest son, Gregory, is twelve years old, and suffers from Poliomyelitis, a debilitating disease which causes the death of nerve cells in the spine or the brain, and is inoperable, the disease can sometimes be stopped in its tracks, but it is not always successful. I talk to my Son as often as I can by the radio I keep in the anchor chain hold. I do this as discreetly as I can, and more especially, if I think I may not see him Ever again. Hence my disappearance when the ship is under attack from the enemy. MY ENEMY.

I will continue to do this if I am able, for as long as am alive. It may even seem selfish of me, to appear like I am running away when under attack, but I will not sacrifice my child's expectations of talking to me, in what could be my last opportunity.

Over to you gentlemen. Oh, Tea or Coffee? I've asked my steward to oblige. Geordie!"

The so-called Captain's Steward turned out to be Taff's second in command, Geordie who he had detailed off to clean up the wardroom, etc. The steward laid the tray on the table containing the coffee and tea etc. Looking at Dave Summers's face, he said, "Sorry chief, I couldn't tell you, now could I?" He said I'll have a chat later OK?"

"Yes you will my Geordie friend."

Roland Evans was sitting at the table with a perplexed look, "So you've known all of this from day one?" he said to Royce "But you didn't think to tell me anything about the intentions. Are they the company intentions or are they the navy's intentions?

or have I got to make it up as I go along?"

"I have a lot of questions to answer Roland, and I would rather it if you and I could sit down together and discuss this man to man, I must tell you all, however, that we will sail from Malta tonight, we will slip away quietly at 23:30, bound for the Suez Canal. That's all I will say at the moment, except, return to your duties and prepare the ship for sea.

With that the Captain stood up, with the intention it seemed, of dismissing the three officers.

"Right now then Captain," Said the Chief Engineer, "You may think this little chat is over? . . . I can assure you it is Far from finished. I have ordered the crew, including all officers, to assemble on the deck hatch at 10:00h. This was before our little chat here in your cabin. You will kindly address the ships company as Captain at that time, and assure them that those who wished to leave could do so. If I am to believe your previous intention, the crew must be given that option, and it must be made clear that their wages would be paid before they leave the ship. Whatever other information you wish to give, will be your choice.

But, be aware that the whole ship's company will probably follow my advice rather than trust what you may say. Is that clear Captain?"

"Whatever we may both say at this point, will be down to the crew's decision I believe Chief and there is the difficult decision to make as to what transport they may be able to get from Malta back home?"

"Well, the crew will muster in 20 minutes, Captain. I'll see you on the upper deck.

Evans turned and followed the First Officer and the Steward from the room. They retired to the wardroom and went straight to the coffee pot.

After the Captain's chat and the Chief Engineers address

to him in his cabin, all three officers sat quietly in the ward-room for at least ten minutes before someone spoke first, and that was Taff Summers.

"I don't think the crew have much option in the present circumstance, do you Roland or you Phillip? It looks like a closed book to me."

Phillip chirped in "I think you are probably right Taff. Any one of the crew who thought about it, would have no idea how to go about getting home for a start, let alone paying for it. Let's not get ahead of ourselves, we all know what the trip down was like in the Atlantic, and it would be just as bad going back up, so the options are very limited. Let's wait and see what the old man says."

Looking at his watch, Evans stood up and said "It's time to face the music anyway now. Let's go"

They went out onto the hatch deck, where the whole crew were already assembled waiting for the Captain to appear. When he did appear he was dressed in his best Uniform with medals etc. He looked very smart indeed.

"Gentlemen, we will say a little prayer before we begin, please remove your headgear."

Then he began his prayer . . .

"Dear Lord, Grant us the serenity, to accept the things we cannot change, the courage to change the things we can. And the wisdom to know the difference Amen. You may replace your headgear. Thank you."

Then he began his speech . . .

"We have spent the past months on a perilous journey to help our fellow man in distress. On our way, South, a lot of our comrades have given their lives to save the lives of others. We, on board this ship, have not lost one soul, Thank God. We now have an opportunity to proceed with our next objective; that is to sail to Africa via The Suez Canal. After the canal, we challenge the Red Sea, go on past Aden and into The Indian Ocean, we will then be going south down the Indian Ocean to Beira in Mozambique, to pick up a cargo which will await us, before we continue on to Cape Town. The journey should take about six to eight weeks weather – and "The Hun" permitting."

There was a murmuring in the rank of sailors.

"He'll be bloody lucky," said a voice in the assembled company "It'll take us that long just to get to Cape-Town" another voice piped in.

Royce chose to ignore the remarks, and went on,

"We will re-fuel at the Naval Base in Simons Town, we will be allowed to do that because of our journey to Malta with the Royal Navy, we will also get some respite there, and some relaxation for a short time. Two or three days maybe. Then we head for home. That is all gentlemen, thank you and dismiss. Will the ship's officers kindly retire to my state-room on dismissal please"

With that, Royce turned and left the loading deck, and the ship's company dispersed to their workplaces, while the officers followed the Captain to his stateroom as he called it. When the officers entered the Captain's stateroom, they were flabbergasted to see the large dining table laid out with sandwiches, cakes and other goodies including bottles of wine and decanters of whiskey, etc. awaiting their pleasure. When all the officers were inside, the Captain stood at the end of the table.

"Gentlemen," he said "This spread has no doubt been a big surprise. But I wanted to Reward you all, for your devotion to this ship's safety from enemy attack, and other feats of courage you have carried out since we left Southampton all those long months ago. At long last, I have seen the light – so to speak – and realised that there is more friendship, bravery, and comradeship in this ship than I knew. That is because I have another family here on board my own ship. Please help yourselves, and thank Geordie for his effort.

They all tucked in and got on with general chatter. The Captain was walking around the room making polite conversation with his crew, most of whom had not spoken to him at all since they joined the ship. The Captain also went out of his way to talk to the young Cadets, who all seemed to appreciate the honour. It turned out to be a very pleasant hour in the Captain's company for everyone. Very unexpected, and Very different to the normal situation which usually ensued.

They all retired to their own parts of the ship, that is, the area where they worked. That last day in Malta had given everyone on board a different outlook on things to come. It seemed to be more pleasant since the morning talk and the invitation to the Captain's cabin.

CHAPTER 4

The Bermuda Star slipped quietly out of Grand Harbour, at the appointed time, probably unnoticed in the dark, and made off towards the Eastern end of the Mediterranean and the eventual Suez Canal. It was suggested to the Captain that he should shift his portable transmitter to the Radio Room or even use the ship's radio, to call his son on a regular basis. Which he accepted, with grateful thanks to the Radio Officer for suggesting it. He would now be able to contact his Son from the Radio room on the bridge.

Suddenly life had become easier on board, at least for the time being, though they had a Long journey ahead, and possible enemy attack, but everything at this moment was running smoothly.

They reached Port Said by late evening on the fourth day of their voyage through the Med. They had a short stay-over at Port Said where they refueled and stocked up on water and some victuals, this before their long haul down the Indian Ocean to their next destination Beira, in Mozambique. No one but the Captain knew what cargo they were going to pick up in Beira, most of the crew had no idea what Mozambique produced. Probably sugar or maybe rice? It was thought by some of the Old Salts on board.

Their transit through the Suez Canal was long and boring, most of the crew not actually on watch, were either sleeping in their bunk or stretched out on the deck sunning themselves. After Suez, the long journey through the Red Sea, through the Gulf of Aden and into the Indian Ocean began.

They finally turned the most northerly part of Somalia and into the Indian Ocean, with another thousand – plus miles to go to Beira, where they would pick up the mysterious cargo. It was an uneventful journey down through the Indian Ocean, boring in fact, since they did not see another ship during the journey, apart from a few fishing vessels off the coast of Madagascar. This did seem odd, though; the Mozambique Channel was usually teeming with fishermen's vessels if nothing else. The situation was quite unusual. The Fist Officer had taken over the bridge from his second officer, as was his custom when approaching the ship's destination.

The ship's Captain would also – normally be on the bridge by now as well, but they were several hours away from accepting a Pilot, and the second officer had gone to prepare the ship for harbour. A normal procedure.

Phillip Rogers, could not understand why the area was so quiet, he had transited this area, before the war began even when he was a young second officer. It seemed a bit odd though; he remembered the last time he came down this coast; it was very busy. He called his young officer cadet, one of the three learners, "Anthony, go and seek out the Chief Engineer for me. Ask him, if he can spare a few moments, could he come to the bridge to see me, tell him I'm very sorry to ask, but it is important."

"Right," Sir and the young officer said, and went to find the Chief Engineer.

About ten minutes later Chief Evans appeared.

"This is an unusual call Phillip; I was about to go to the engine room. What's the Problem? "Roland, I'm sorry to have asked you to come up, but would you say that this area, which I know you are familiar with; is – well, very quiet? It would normally be teeming with fishing boats and the like, do you think there could be something not quite right. I don't know why, but I've got this strange feeling."

"Well, it does seem to be quiet Phillip I agree, but it is getting late in the day, It's what – coming up 17:00", he said, "what are you concerned about?"

"Well normally, wouldn't you say, there would be quite a few fishing boats at least, around at this time, and possibly, other vessels which would also be ending the day around now. I don't know why, but I have a strange feeling something is not right."

"Well I admit it is quiet, but I wouldn't have said there was anything to worry about. We are, what; about four hours off? But thinking about it, it does seem a bit quiet; Beira is not such a busy port now I shouldn't think, what with the war and everything. I'll go and have a word with the Captain; he made the arrangements for a pick-up here; He might have a clue why it's so quiet. Slow the ship right down to five knots or so. If that doesn't bring him to the bridge nothing will."

The First Officer did exactly what the Chief engineer told him to do, and within minutes, the Captain appeared on the bridge.

"What's happening Mr. Rogers, have we got a Pilot so soon?"

"No Captain," said Rogers.

"I am a bit concerned about the lack of shipping in the area. It does appear to be extremely quiet for such a normally, busy Port. I was wondering if the port might be under the control of the Germans by now, it would not surprise me.

I heard recently on the radio that German Patrol boats have been attacking villages on the river at Zambia. And now, possibly, they have taken over areas in Mozambique. Maybe even Beira. What do you think Captain?"

"Utter rubbish Phillip, when we left Malta the Port at Beira was bustling with shipping, that is why I undertook this assignment, it was also to repay the fine crew we have aboard this vessel, who took the ship to Malta under severe conditions."

The Chief engineer now intervened.

"Captain Royce. I think you should listen to your First Officer before you dismiss what he has just pointed out.

I should tell you that I or the ship's company have not yet heard a word of our supposed cargo to be picked up here in Beira. Before you even think about picking up an unknown cargo, you should contact Malta Communications centre and ask for advice from our very good friend Captain Trail. He will no doubt give you the advice, you so obviously need, about the enemy situation in this area before you sacrifice this Ship, and her company to the ENEMY, because that is who we are up against. Do you understand that?"

"Yes I understand, but you, Chief engineer, have no authority to interfere in matters of ship handling. It Is "I," The Captain, who is in complete command of this ship, and the crew will accept my authority or face the consequences. Now – step aside.

First Officer Rogers. Step aside also, and be aware, you

will go before a company tribunal to answer for your insubor-dination and insulting behaviour in front of crew members."

Royce seemed to be spluttering uncontrollably and fuming in a rage, to all on the bridge.

The Chief engineer stepped forward again.

"Mr. Royce, YOU will stand aside from the bridge, I am The most senior man on this ship; I forbid you to sacrifice this crew to the enemy; and, if it is your intention to carry out this foolish escapade, I will exercise my authority as second in command of this vessel and have you arrested, and confined to your quarters until I!, sail this ship to Simons town, where you will be charged with being a traitor to your country, and face the probability of a court martial. First Officer Rogers, return this man to his cabin. He is to be locked in and a guard put by his cabin door until we reach Simons town."

Two men were detailed, and the Captain was escorted to his cabin as ordered, protesting like a young child. Royce was wrestling with the two sailors who were trying to get him to his cabin. They finally got him into his room and shut and locked the door, handing the key to Summers. OK lads, leave this with me, go back to your duties. I'll handle him now. Thanks.

"Captain, this is the chief steward. I'm going to open the door and come in.

Don't even try to rush me because you will lose the fight, just be calm, and I will talk to you like I always do. Now stand away from the door as I enter."

He put the key in the lock and pushed the door open; he was not sure what would happen, but he walked into the room and saw the Captain standing by the table. Summers put the key back in the lock but didn't turn it shut.

"Now then, why is it all of a sudden you go crazy again. I think you know more than you are telling, about this cargo. It is my belief that you are hiding the truth behind this cargo business, that is also what Mr. Evans thinks. I think you should now put your trust in both Mr. Evans, Mr. Rogers, and me, and tell us Exactly what sort of trouble you are in. The alternative, of course, is that you will regret your actions if you even try, to get to the Germans in Beira. Your efforts with the story about your son, are absolute rubbish of course. You don't think we were fooled by your pathetic efforts to cover up your disappearances by such a story as phoning your Son from the cable Locker, because you do not have a Son, neither do you have a wife anymore. She left you five years ago when she found out about your affair with another woman. I won't mention her name because she was also conned by your pathetic efforts to go to Germany, because she was a German, and you thought that through her, you could be accepted into the German Navy. But of course you didn't know at the time that she was, in fact, Jewish, and she would not return to Germany under any circumstance.

I've been waiting for years to put you in a compromising situation Royce so that you could be caught out, and now you have been. You forget how long I've known you, in fact, you must know that you have no secrets that you can hide from me,"

"Don't think you have the better of me Mr. Summers. I have a lot of German friends who are actually waiting for me in Beira. They acknowledged receipt of my message, from my radio; still in the cable locker incidentally, and I sent a message to them again early this morning giving them our ETA. Don't be surprised if you see a ship coming for me before long."

"I won't be, because it will be a British Warship, and you will surely hang."

Summers then turned and left the room. He shut the Captain's door and locked it, and then found a screwdriver to put through the handle." "Now get out of that he said to himself."

When Summers returned to the bridge, the Chief Engineer and the First Officer were still there, with Mr. Watts now at the helm. Several other crew members had also assembled on the bridge to find out what was going on.

"News travels fast Taff," said Evans, nodding toward the people who were crowding the bridge, everyone on board was anxious to know what was going on.

"Philip and I have decided we will carry on down to Simons town before we intercept any of Herr Royce's German friends. So here we go."

He turned to the overcrowded bridge,

"OK lads, clear the bridge and give Mr. Watts some breathing space.

Right then, Port thirty Mr. Watts", said the First Officer "full ahead both engines, Let's make for Simons-town. We should make it in about two and a half days, with luck, somebody ask the chief chef to delay dinner till seven o clock, give us a chance to get well under way before they come rolling out after us."

"OK Boss all done" said one of the seamen.

The Bermuda Star had covered a great deal of sea area since they left Southampton. They had been very lucky they had come so far without mishap. They were now heading south for South Africa and hopefully a bit of respite. They had been away from home for a long time, and most were missing wives and sweethearts, Mums and Dads. But for most of the crew the thing they missed most was mail. Letters from home. They had not received any mail from home since they left Southampton, not even at Malta, due to the tremendous bombing the island had been subjected to, they thought they would not receive any at all now because no one knew where they were.

The radio officer, sensing this disappointment, stepped in with some good news to cheer them up, the news that he had forwarded all mail for the ship, via the Forces Post Office system, to Simons town Naval Base, and it would be waiting for them when they arrived. This prompted a little cheer, followed by Mr. Watts comment . . .

"OK you lot, now clear my? bridge, before I run onto a sandbank."

They all gave a little laugh at George's comments, but left the bridge in a better frame of mind.

"Right, now Chief engineer, what kind of speed can you give us?" asked Phillip Rogers. "Maybe 24 – 25 knots" He said with a smile "but probably 20 knots with a bit of push. In fact, I don't care if burn the old girl out, so long as she gets us to Simons town" Evans said with a smile.

"Don't burn her out Chief, not until were tied up alongside anyway!" so said George Watts.

There were four of them left on the bridge, and the steward pointed out that he had chained the Captain's cabin door, "but we still need to keep an eye on him, not knowing what he can get up to. We don't know if he's got his own radio transmitter with him or not. I know he didn't want it to be put in the Wireless room." "He told me he still had it in the cable locker, and that he'd passed a message to the Germans stating what our intentions are. We'll also have to keep an eye on him in case he finds a way of getting out,

It's a big porthole in his cabin, and nothing would surprise me of his capability, he's fooled us all one way or another. I think we ought to check the porthole.

I'll get one of the seamen over the side, just to make sure it's secure."

"Don't bother with that." said Evans "That porthole was sealed inside and outside during the short refit, it was smashed in when we entered the dry dock in Portsmouth. The Old man blamed the tug of course; It had to be repaired during the docking. The company were not pleased. Apart from the delay, it cost them dearly. Another whole day in fact. That porthole is secure I'm pretty sure of that. Although it was about five years ago when we had that re-fit, anyway let's not worry about that now."

"Right then, let's get this show on the road, as they say in the films," said Rogers, "I want to be in Simons town in at least two and a half days – with a bit of luck. I hope the chefs have done their job and we can eat. I'm starving. Mr. Watts, I'll get you a relief to have a meal, but I'd like you to do a couple of extra watches at the helm. You'll have me for company for most of the time. I'll be sending a few lookout's up top to the Crow's nest. I'll be putting one hand on the bow and one on the stern as well. This is unknown waters to us, and we need to keep a sharp lookout for anything suspicious. I believe we are in German territory, and we need to be on the Alert at all times, and that's why I want you on the bridge Mr. Watts. Your experience in handling the ship in difficult situations is invaluable."

"Yes! Thank you, Mr. Rogers. To save any problems with look-outs, perhaps you could get the chef to bring me a dinner here on the bridge. That should save time in placing the look-outs in their places etc. I have no problems with that. Tell the chef I'd like a nice mug of tea, as well as the mug he sends up with my dinner?"

"I'll do that Mr" Watts. Is there anything else?"

"Not unless he's got this morning's paper with the racing results in thank you, sir."

"Right then George – I'll see if I can carry out your order to the TEA"

Rogers left the bridge with a smile on his face at George Watts's sense of humour. It was now coming up to about 19:35, and most of the ship's company were getting ready to go to their watch stations. It was going to be a long two and a half days before they would reach Simonstown – maybe longer. but they all knew by now what was expected of each man on board.

To quote the Captain's speech at their departure from Southampton, and Lord Nelson? of course. "England expects ETC."

Mr. Watts had his dinner and a nice big cup of tea brought to the bridge by the head chef himself.

"Here you are George, Saville Row service. You can't fault it, can you?

"Thanks, Burt, that's good of you."

"No trouble at all George. Most of the lads are gone to lookout stations and whatever else. Any idea when we are likely to get to Simons town?"

"Hopefully in a couple of days, but that don't mean a thing, the First Officer thinks maybe two and a half days. Personally, I think it's more than three plus days. It's longer than Mr. Rogers thinks."

"You bin ere before then George? I've never been down this way. I've been to the Far East mind you, a good few times before the war started. We used to go to Ceylon a lot at one time. We always had a good cup a tea there."

"Yea, those were days, when we were young Eh? Little darlings in grass skirts and nothing else, showering you with coconut milk and fruit from the vine."

"Hang on George, don't get carried away. But they were happier times back then. Ah well!" They were both looking out to sea through the glass screen, thinking of days gone by.

"Ah well," said Burt again "Better get back to the Galley or you lot will have no breakfast."

At that moment a loud explosion occurred, it seemed to be up forward by the Fore Peak, where the anchor chain was stowed.

"What in hell – were being attacked by those Gerry's in a submarine" Watts shouted. He turned the wheel hard to port; it seemed that was where they had been hit, and suddenly the whole ship was alive with men running to their battle stations.

The gun, left by the Navy, was still on the bridge deck of course but had not been used by the gunners since they entered Malta, and the ammunition for it had been stored in ammunition boxes in the hold.

Suddenly the bridge was full of people, including the engineer. The First Officer arrived within a minute and took command of the situation.

"Someone go and release the Captain from his cabin. Is Mr. Summers here?" He shouted.

"Yes, Sir I'm here. I'll go and let the Captain out."

The Chief Steward left and went to release the Captain.

When he got to the Captain's cabin, the door had been opened, and the Captain had disappeared. Summers thought immediately of the anchor cable stowage. It was the first thing that came into his head. He went inside the cabin, and the first thing he looked for was the porthole on the starboard side of the room. There it was. Exactly as it should have been, secured shut, and could not be opened. He turned to go back out of the cabin, thinking that the Captain had gone somewhere else on the ship, and he should look for him.

"Chief Steward" Summers spun around "Captain, how did you open the door?"

"My secret," He said with a sly grin "What are you all doing about the submarine attack."

"Are you responsible for this? Summers asked.

"How can I be, I've been locked up in here for two days? But you should be aware by now that the Enemy – that is the German Navy! – will not allow you to get away easily.

They will destroy this ship and all who stay on board, but I know they will give you all a chance to take to the boats, and I suggest you do so now before It's too late. They have given you a warning shot, now take advantage; and abandon the ship.

I would like to thank you Mr. Summers for being my steward for all these years, and though you may not believe it, you have been a friend, in fact, the only friend I've had all these years. Now make haste and, get the boats away before they start shooting again. I have to check my Ship before they destroy it completely."

He pushed past the steward in haste and disappeared up the hatchway to the deck.

Dave Summers was at a complete loss. He could not believe what he had just seen, nor could he have stopped the Captain brushing past him. He dashed back to the bridge, took hold of the Chief engineer's arm and took him aside.

"He's got out of his cabin, and no, not through the port-hole, through his cabin door – I don't know how he did it, but he is obviously aware that the enemy are going to sink the ship, and has advised that we abandon, immediately, before they start shelling seriously. I honestly think you should be doing as he advised before we all die on board. And I'm not being dramatic Roland. This bloke is seriously demented."

"How in hell did he get out? I think perhaps we should take heed, and get the men off. I realised that he is in League with the Germans. How I obviously don't know. I'll get the men to lower the boats. You go round and check everyone is aware that we abandon ship NOW" Evans set off the alarm on the bridge and broadcast to the ship.

"This is the Chief Engineer Speaking. ABANDON SHIP – ABANDON SHIP. All hands to the lifeboats. Abandon Ship Now"

He turned to the helmsman George Watts. "That means you too George. Signal stop engines, then get to the boats. Good luck mate" and he shook hands with the helmsman.

"Typical this," said George "I haven't had dinner yet – I don't suppose the chef will think of taking a picnic hamper. Ah well. I'll see you on the other side Roland" and he left the bridge.

Roland could not help smiling; it was typical of George to make a joke of the situation. He was one of life's characters, especially at sea.

He was now on the bridge alone. He then headed down to the engine room, to make sure his team had heard the alarm to abandon and had shut down the engines. As he was leaving the bridge, Phillip Rogers appeared.

"Roland, thank God you're OK, come with me – Now! I want you to get into the boats, and don't argue. Tom Taylor has shut down and checked everyone is out, nothing for you to worry about down in your precious engine room, so please get in the boat What about the Captain. Have you seen him, And Dave Summers? Has he got on the boats."

"Everyone is getting on the lifeboats. Come on I'm not leaving you behind."

"I've got to check the engine room," Evans said again.

"No need Roland everything has been checked and the engine room is clear, engines shut down, and crew all accounted for – now please come with me and get in the lifeboat." Rogers took Roland by the arm and escorted him to the lifeboat; it was the last of the lifeboats on board.

Evans was still protesting when he was forced down the into the boat.

As they pulled away, Evans saw Royce standing on the bridge deck alongside the Gun, which they had never used in anger since they left Malta. The lifeboats had pulled away from the ship when suddenly a gun opened up behind them. It was, of course, the submarine, which had at least given them a chance to avoid the line of fire and get away to a reasonable distance. Perhaps Royce did have some influence with his German (friends?).

The lifeboats had pulled away past the stern of Bermuda Star, and were now out of the line of fire as the submarine began its destruction of the ship.

"Phillip. Did you make a check of all the crew who entered the lifeboats?" asked Roland Evans. "Which boat did the chief steward get into?"

"I saw him giving George Watts a hand to get him into the second boat, Roland. It looked like George was struggling, and Taff was having a bit of trouble getting him in. I don't know If he'd been hit or not, but Taff Summers definitely took him to the lifeboat and helped him."

"Yeah I saw Taff helping George, and he did look like he'd been hit," said one of the other crew members.

Meanwhile, the submarine was constantly bombarding the ship, to the extent that – suddenly, an explosion ripped the ship, and a fierce fire took hold, which seemed to spread in minutes. As the three lifeboats watched, the ship suddenly blew up from amidships, and into the sky like a volcanic eruption. Thank goodness all three lifeboats had got away far enough, to avoid the falling debris. Those crew members in the lifeboats who saw the ship blow up, all had different views of life on board the old Bermuda Star. Some were glad they had got away because they were not happy on board. Others were Nostalgic, and some of the crew had been with the ship for many years, and to them, it was home. However, no one had expected to find themselves as a cast-away in the Indian Ocean. It was an unknown situation, especially for the young cadets.

"An experience you will never forget most likely. assuming you ever get home to tell the story."

Quoted one of the old salt's in the lifeboat.

"A proper Job's comforter story,"

One of the other crew members remarked.

"Don't take any notice of him boys. I got a message away to Simons town radio office before we had to take to the boats, and they got our message" said the Radio Officer.

"Well done Sparks," said one of the other seniors in the boat.

"Can anybody see any of the other boats? said the engineer.

"Yes chief, they're all a good way out now. I don't think we should try to catch up with anyone just yet, the further apart we are, the more likely we are to avoid being attacked. I think we should just carry on as we are maybe until daylight."

"You are probably right Phillip. Good thinking. I should leave the Captain's job to the Captain in future eh?"

"It might save a lot of misunderstanding Roland," said Phillip with a smile.

The submarine had been firing ammunition at the ship, for most of the time since the lifeboat's getaway. Suddenly, the whole ship exploded in a shower of smoke and flame which flew high into the sky and fell back into the sea, to disappear into the depths of the Indian Ocean. Everyone in the lifeboats gasped in horror at the sight the ship's destruction. Almost in one deadly explosion, she was no more. Whereas the bright fire from the previous explosion had lit up the ocean, the second turned the night sky into a darkened abyss it seemed. The three boats lifted their oars across the gunwales and sat there in the dark wondering what would happen next.

Would the submarine come after them, would German surface ships find them and sink them in their lifeboats. The last person to leave the ship was the first officer, escorting the chief engineer. There was no telling at this time if everyone on board had managed to get into the lifeboats.

Phillip Rogers decided, (To himself), that as soon as it was daylight, he would try and catch up with the other two lifeboats and make a check of who had got away. The one person who he could discount was, of course, The Captain, who was seen on the bridge by most of the crew already in the lifeboats. He had been standing by the Gun on the port side of the bridge when the submarine was firing at the ship. It was obvious that he had "Gone Down" with his ship.

By the time dawn broke, they had rowed quite a few miles away from the scene of the Bermuda Star's destruction and were on the lookout for the two other lifeboats. Phillip

Rogers calculated that they must be about twenty-five to thirty miles from shore. There was a heavy swell, which made it almost impossible to spot any other vessels at all, so the likelihood of catching up with either of them seemed; not out of the question, but maybe difficult.

He sought out the survival kit on board, and passed water around to everyone. "You all realise that we have a limited survival kit onboard the lifeboat, so I'll just remind you all of the rules. I will dish out water and hardtack once a day. It is my belief that we are not far from friendly waters if that's so then it should not be long before we come across a friendly face. So don't think of the worst way – think of the best way to overcome our present situation, and that is, of course, a good old British "Stiff upper lip." To which the whole boat laughed out loud.

"Well said, Captain! Let's get on with it lads. Put your back's into it." said the Chef "It'll be steaks all round when I can find a galley."

"That'll be the day," said the usual misery – (one is found in every ship.)

"OK, then lads let's get our backs into it and head south, rather than try and get ashore on this coast. We don't know what were up against up here, so let's get to Simons town. We should be able to last out for a few days and more if the weather allows. OK back's into it give way together" The six rowers currently pulling, heaved together and they moved off.

It was difficult with the heavy swell coming at them broadside on, but they got into pulling together eventually. It was not an easy way to row in such a heavy swell. They tried rowing diagonally to Starboard, and then again diagonally to Port. Each time, the boat was getting swamped, and there was a danger that they might capsize. Phillip Rogers decided to turn seaward and attempt to see if he could overcome the incoming waves. It would seem that if they did this, the swell would be less fierce, the further away from the shore they went, they were now about fifteen miles from the beach. The turn itself was hair-raising enough, but they managed to face the oncoming sea safely, and it did turn out to be the right thing to do, but a bit hairy in the execution.

There was less chance now of meeting up with the two other boats, so the First Officer decided to tell his own boatload what he thought. "Right lads, I think the situation we face could be one of two chances we have before us. One, we can carry on south as far as we are able, here in the hope that we can reach Cape-town, Or if we think we could do better by going ashore and heading south on foot? The first one to speak was the Chief Engineer.

"We will never make it on land. I know it is an option Phillip, but we have more chance of being picked up here at sea. Don't forget the Royal Navy will be up and down this coast patrolling for Enemy shipping. We have more chance of being picked up here, than being in a wilderness ashore."

"Yes, that's the best option Mr. Rogers" the youngest Radio Officer Piped in who's usual statements received a kick in the posterior from his boss. However he was determined to have his say "My Father, who was an Admiral in the R.N. told me when I was just a boy at school, that you're safer at sea in a storm than stuck in the sand in a desert sand storm."

"Well said young-un. See boss, out of the mouth of babes"? said his boss, the radioman, and the whole crew had a chuckle at the youngster's remark.

"Thank you Simon Junior," said the First Officer. We will acknowledge both the Admiral and the Chief Engineer for their advice.

Now then I think the sea-swell has settled enough for us to go south, and try our luck." They rowed in watches of an hour each man, in an attempt to conserve energy. They rowed through day one into day two and into day three, by which time they were running short of water and food. Day three dawned bright and became hotter as the day went on, challenging the energy of all on board. They were resting more often now as the rowing became harder most of the crew were by now, resting either across the oars or lying on the gunwales, or even on their opposite number. The First Officer had not left the helm steerage since they left the ship. He slept quick naps, but all the time he was fully aware of his responsibility to his crew. The young radio officer Simon was the first to notice what could be a ship on the horizon. He discretely directed the Captain's attention, so as not to arouse too much attention, in case it was, perhaps an enemy ship. Mr. Rogers then alerted the crew.

"Right lads. Wake up all of you. There is a ship on the horizon, heading this way by the look of it. She could be the enemy, or she could be our saviour. Whoever she is, friend or foe, we might still get a cup of water each?"

"Hurrah" shouted the crew as one.

It turned out she was a British warship, HMS Starling. As she got closer to them, it seemed a number of people were standing on the bow; and sure enough, those people turned out to be shipmates from Bermuda Star. There was much cheering and back slapping as they climbed aboard the frigate. Mr. Rogers and Mr. Evans were greeted by the First Lieutenant of Starling and were invited to the Captain's cabin, and were greeted by none other than Commander Thompson. The same man who had been the Gunnery Officer on their way to Malta.

Gentlemen, I'm so glad to see that you are all alive. I know you have lost some of your old Crew, but we have most of them on board now. They had a long story to tell of course, and a story of sorrow to hear, when it was revealed, Chief Steward Dave Summers, and the helmsman Mr. George Watts had been unable to get off the ship before she exploded. We don't know what happened fully, but it is believed that Mr. Watts was injured, and could not get into the lifeboat before a large wave, took it away from the ship's side. The ship had a blazing fire attacking the port side, and nothing could be done to help them. The lifeboat had to get away from the blaze. The blaze was followed by an explosion Dave Summers had stayed by George's, side helping him as best as he could. He also missed the opportunity to save himself It seems. He stood by George through to the end. Not that it is a happy ending, but you may like to know that. The Admiral, who is still in Malta, has recommended them both for a BEM. That is the British Empire Medal; it is a civilian medal for bravery and devotion to the Crown. Their families have been informed. Well now gentlemen, I shall take you back to Simons town with me and hand you over to the Merchant Navy office in Cape town. Meanwhile, it's about time you had a meal. I doubt you have eaten in a good while. My chief steward here will take care of you, and I will meet you later when I hope you have been able to rest up for a few hours. The Captain then gave them over to his chief steward, and he went about his own duties.

It was almost six months later when Phillip Rogers and Roland Evans were able to return to the United Kingdom. Some of the crew members were able to pick up jobs on other ship's that visited Cape-town, and some even went "Native" and got other jobs in the area. The Chief radio officer enlisted in the South African Navy, mostly British at that time. It was published in the UK National Daily Newspapers, that "Captain Royce," in fact, had purchased the ship Bermuda Star, but had not yet paid the previous owners a penny. This was very unfair to the crew who had been working on board the ship, and still in the Merchant Navy but were unaware of the fact that the ship they worked on was not registered under the British Law. They had not been paid a penny either. The British seamanship board finally solved the problem. They were paid for the voyage to Malta only.

Captain Royce was last seen on the Port Side of the bridge looking out towards the lifeboats pulling away from the ship. Those crewmen who saw him were more concerned with trying to rescue Dave Summers and George Watts and get them on the last lifeboat. They were having great difficulty because of the heavy swell constantly dragging the boat away from the attempted rescue.

The ship was being pounded by gunfire from the German submarine and the lifeboat was unable to get to the stricken crewmen off. Suddenly there was a tremendous explosion, which blew the ship out of the water. The lifeboat, trying to rescue Dave and George, was swept away by the heavy swell caused by the explosion.

The crew kept rowing madly to save everyone else in the boat from the falling debris, and to prevent the boat capsizing.

Later, after the ship's crew had been rescued by the Navy. It had been assumed that the Captain, who was last seen on the bridge, had "Gone down" with his ship.

However; later information proved that Royce was never

the honourable Captain, who had "Gone down" with his ship. He had been picked up by the enemy submarine before the final explosion sank the which Bermuda Star.

www.ingramcontent.com/pod-product-compliance
Lightning Source LLC
Chambersburg PA
CBHW020627130626
46552CB00003B/1113